Broken Dolls

BROKEN Dolls

KITTY THOMAS

Burlesque Press

Printed in the United States of America

ISBN-13: 978-1-938639-19-7
ISBN-10: 1-938639-19-7

Wholesale orders can be placed through Ingram.
Published by Burlesque Press

contact: burlesquepress@nym.hush.com

For M.

Acknowledgments

Thank you to the following people for their help with Broken Dolls:

Robin Ludwig @ gobookcoverdesign.com for the amazing cover art as always! You are my lobster!

Michelle for editing help. Thank you for making time for me!

Thanks to M for proofreading, digital formatting, and for being generally awesome. Love you!

Frankie the cat for her disapproving looks when I tried to play with Legos when I was supposed to be working.

Disclaimer

This is a work of fiction, and neither the publisher nor the author endorse or condone any actions carried out by any fictional character in this work or any other. This work is intended for an emotionally mature adult audience.

Author's Note:

This book takes places in the same world as Guilty Pleasures. It is not necessary to have read Guilty Pleasures to enjoy Broken Dolls, however, if you have read Guilty Pleasures, the events of Broken Dolls (after the prologue) begin 3 years after the end of that book.

Prologue

"**G**et out, you fucking whore!"

Mina scrambled to wrap herself in the bed sheet. She dove for the ground as a vase smashed, dumping shards of glass into her long dark hair.

"If I'm a whore, it's only because you threw me down on my knees in front of your friends, chortling about what a good little submissive slut I was!"

Shut up. He's going to kill you if you don't shut up.

She was still bleeding from Jason's whip. Why rile him more now?

"You dare speak to your master this way?"

She cringed as he raised his hand. "I-I'm sorry. Please."

He wasn't her master. He wasn't her fucking anything. It was a game they'd played. A game she'd played with other men before him. And it always ended here. How could this be right? How could this be normal if it always ended in abuse?

Surely Jason had cured her of the last vestiges of whatever fucked-up sexual fantasies swirled inside her head. This could never be real.

The people she knew in the lifestyle—they were all liars. They must be. What pain were they hiding behind a mask of perfect submission and the ideal dominant who seemed kind yet always in command?

In public anyway. When the parties were over and the doors closed, didn't the masks come off to reveal the twisted truth beneath?

Most relationships weren't ideal. Didn't everybody wear a mask? Wouldn't conflict be that much more explosive inside this type of dynamic? How screwed up was she that she wanted to make herself so vulnerable to the people who always hurt her no matter how much she begged for kindness?

Next week would someone see one of her newest scars? Would Mina insist it was consensual? All to cover up the fact that somehow she'd allowed herself to become this . . . this *thing*.

"You're not a real sub," Jason bellowed, as he ate up the space between them in two long strides. His face was red and contorted in rage. The official insult of abusive dominants everywhere: *You're not a real sub.*

How many times had he said this now? How many times had she forced herself to stay to try to prove to him that she was good? That she was real. That she was worth more.

His large hand wrapped around her throat, squeezing. And for a moment, everything that had ever happened in her life rushed out in a sprawling pointless vision before her. One long fucked-up slide show of pleasure and pain.

"I want you and all your shit out of my apartment. If I come home from the gym tomorrow and I find any of it or you still here, what happened tonight will look like a romantic candlelit dinner. Do you understand me?"

"I don't have a job. You made me quit. I have nowhere to go." Was she begging him to keep her?

Oh God. She was. There were nothing left of her. One small piece at a time had been traded out while she'd hardly noticed . . . and now . . . she didn't recognize any of it. She didn't recognize herself.

"Maybe you should have taken your role with me more seriously. I'm sure you'll find a new dick to suck by tomorrow evening."

He released her throat and moved to the opposite end of the room as if he couldn't trust himself mere feet from her. Mina trembled as she tried to keep herself covered. Maybe it was shock. She wasn't sure. All she knew was that no matter how many times he'd seen her naked, she couldn't stand to let him see her again—not when he was like this. All she felt when he looked at her now was shame.

"I was honest," she said. "I told you what I needed, that I was looking for someone gentle. I didn't hold anything back."

Jason jerked open a drawer and threw clothes at her. She struggled to catch them before they hit the ground.

His expression turned dark. "I don't give a fuck what you need. You agreed to be mine. There's something inside you, Mina, that makes people want to hurt you. You'll never find a man who'll be gentle."

One

10 Months Later

Gainful employment had been the easy part. The hard part was trying to live with herself and the memories of the things she'd allowed Jason and those before him to do to her. Maybe *allowed* wasn't right. What power had she had with him so much stronger than her? Especially all the times he'd tied her down—as if the power differential wasn't frightening enough without ropes or chains.

Mina sat on a sofa outside her therapist's office on the tenth floor. He'd given her the codes so she wouldn't have to wait outside in the frigid cold.

She'd been chain-smoking for the past fifteen minutes waiting for him to arrive. She'd found Dr. Lindsay Smith while looking for a kink-friendly therapist. She'd been searching for someone she could talk to about all of this, someone who might reassure her that she wasn't broken beyond repair. She'd wanted someone who would make her believe that kink was okay—she'd just been unlucky with her partners.

She'd been surprised Lindsay wasn't a woman and had almost bolted that first meeting six months ago.

She'd needed a woman to talk to—not another man—
not some man who would only be kind to her until he'd
managed to get inside her. But so far, Dr. Smith hadn't
made any attempts to fuck her, and his mask of kindness
had yet to slip. Maybe he was her unicorn.

The front door opened. Dr. Smith wore a tailored
dark pinstripe suit and seemed to glide into the building
on a cloud of authority.

"Have you been waiting long?"

She gestured to the five half-smoked cigarettes in the
tray, each with her siren red lipstick print on it. When
she got like this, she couldn't make it through a whole
cigarette before she was snubbing it out and compuls-
ively lighting another. She'd convinced herself that first
inhalation was the best. It brought the deepest calm.
After a few minutes she became impatient with anything
less and lit another.

"I see," he said, grimly. "Give me a moment."

It was Sunday—a day he didn't normally see patients.
It felt weird to be here without the buffer of someone else
in the reception area.

The doctor was in his fifties, judging by the salt and
pepper gray at his temples and the lines on his face. He
had a calm, commanding presence—exactly the type of
man she'd fantasized about finding but didn't think could
be real. He was probably too old for her, but in shape and
good looking. Mina was embarrassed to admit even
inside her own mind that she'd masturbated to many
fantasies of him.

Her previous masters had been closer to her own age.
Maybe it was age. Maybe an older guy, someone like Dr.
Smith wouldn't be . . . She shook herself out of the
thought. He would be like all the others. And just because

he was a kink-friendly therapist didn't mean he was kinky. Or looking for a partner even if he was.

Stop it. This is what's wrong with you. This is why this keeps happening. Just stop!

The doctor poked his head out. "I'm ready for you, Mina." His voice was a deep lullaby, and she found herself coaxed the few steps into his exotic, plant-filled sanctuary.

"No smoking around the orchids," he reminded her gently.

Mina snubbed out her sixth half-smoked cigarette, reapplied her lipstick, straightened her long black pencil skirt, and crossed the threshold. Even at the emotional level she was at, she'd dressed for him. She couldn't bring herself to let him see her in sweatpants with her hair in disarray. She was already about to blubber and cry all over him. There was no need to be even more pathetic.

His inner office was part of what kept her coming back. For all her hesitance about him not being a female doctor, his office created a safe space that few other places did for her anymore. The walls were a soothing lavender to match the orchids that lined the wall. The dark oak desk and coffee table were the only things that kept the room masculine.

Lindsay bypassed the coffeemaker and put some water on to boil in a tea kettle, then he pulled out a notebook and flipped to a fresh page.

"Another nightmare?"

Mina nodded. Her hand shook as she swiped the tears off her cheeks. Shouldn't all this feel *less* traumatic by now? Instead of more? She'd been able to cope just as long as she could deny how bad it had been.

He scribbled a few notes. "Tell me about it."

"I-it's always the same dream. You know the dream." She couldn't bring herself to say it out loud again. He must have twenty pages of notes by now on just this one dream—Jason abusing her in front of his friends. He whipped her, cut her, put out cigarettes on her, then he passed her around. Each time she woke, she could feel the blood running down her back. Each time she panicked and thought it was still happening, but it was only sweat.

It would be so simple if it were just a dream, but it had happened. The worst part was that she hadn't left him that night. She'd stayed until he'd kicked her out months later.

"You've gone a while without the dream," the doctor commented as he flipped back several pages. "What do you think triggered it this time?"

"I went on a date."

"With someone in the lifestyle? Do you think that's wise, given your track record with men?"

Mina looked up sharply. Was he blaming her now? It sounded like a softer echo of Jason's words—as if it was her fault men had beaten her, like there was something fundamentally broken that lured only dangerous animals to her door.

But she didn't have the energy to lash out. And in truth, she was afraid to. What if the doctor hurt her, too? He felt like her last hope in the world. If he turned on her, she wouldn't be able to leave her apartment again.

"N-no. It w-wasn't someone in the lifestyle. It was just a regular guy."

"Did he hurt you?"

She shook her head. "I'm not going out with him again. He wouldn't understand my weirdness. It wouldn't work." She left unspoken the fear that he might hurt her, too.

Tony had seemed perfectly nice. He hadn't done anything to set off warning bells. And he was a cousin of a friend of hers. That made him not a totally random and unknown element.

"Maybe you should be single for a while," Lindsay said.

"I've been single for ten months. I'm broken. I can't do kink. I can't do vanilla. I can't be with anybody without having nightmares, but I'm so lonely I can't breathe."

Lindsay passed a box of tissues across the desk as her tears started to spill over again.

"What do you want, Mina?"

She looked at the crumbled tissues in her hands. "You know what I want. But it doesn't exist. I don't do well on my own, but I do even worse with somebody. All I want, all I've ever wanted is to live in a kink relationship with a gentle master. But it's not real. They all hurt you." Even if it was real, she wasn't sure if she could handle it now. Nobody was going to put up with all her fears or the emotional baggage she'd accumulated.

"That's not true," Lindsay said.

"Well, they all hurt *me*."

"Fair enough."

The doctor stared at an orchid across the room as if he'd entered a fugue state. Several minutes passed before his attention returned to her. He stared intently, as if sizing her up, as if trying to decide something. She looked down again.

Was he about to suggest she be with him? It would break all rules of doctor/patient relationships. It would break the trust they'd already formed. And yet, her heart raced at the idea of being in his house. In his bed.

"What if I told you I could give you the thing you've always craved?"

Mina felt her face flame. He was going there?

"You mean . . .? I-I don't know what you mean." She saved it at the last second. If she said something about the two of them moving into a different type of relationship and that wasn't what he meant, she'd want to die.

He sighed. "I mean, this is not the only work I do. I could match you with someone—A master who would provide for your needs and take care of you. I could ensure he wouldn't harm you. You'd be happy and safe."

"Oh." She hoped her disappointment that he didn't mean him, didn't show.

"Do you want to think about it?"

She should say no. She should just accept a life alone. She'd been doing better until that date with Tony.

"How would you ensure he didn't hurt me?"

"I can't discuss that unless you agree and we get further in the training process. For my own safety."

The warning bells went off. The way he spoke . . . whatever he was suggesting wasn't entirely legal. Maybe not legal at all.

The doctor reviewed his notes. "Would you agree to intercourse with this theoretical master?"

"I, I mean, that's not an option is it? I can't just opt out of that." Even in vanilla relationships she'd known she couldn't just opt out. She'd never liked intercourse. She liked most other sexual acts—or had liked them before Jason—but that one thing was something she just sort of *got through.*

She had no early rape history to blame it on. She'd never had a funny uncle. It just wasn't something she liked, and she couldn't believe she'd told the doctor about that to begin with. It was the kind of thing you never told anybody because *everybody* liked it. And if you didn't, there must be something really wrong with you.

Mina was convinced either other women were lying and faking it, or she'd been broken somehow before anyone ever laid a hand on her.

She couldn't come that way. And sometimes it hurt. And it always gave her a low-level anxiety she couldn't explain. But she'd managed to eroticize the fear to cope and keep going forward. Usually. Most of the time.

Was that the root of her kink? Since the only way to *do sex* was to eroticize fear? She shook the thought from her head. It didn't matter anyway.

"Do you imagine you're the only human being on the planet who isn't fond of that one particular activity?" he asked. "Believe me, I've dealt with all sorts of off-beat tastes, both in dominants and submissives. Nothing surprises me, and this is mild. I could even match you in a non-sexual master/slave relationship if that's what you need and want."

"What would that even look like? I mean, I don't like to be hit. I'm not a masochist at all. Would I just be the guy's maid?" She didn't trust that any man who was attracted to women, who *owned her* would ever be able to not fuck her, let alone not hit her—going on past experience.

"There are all kinds of touch and closeness that isn't sexual. You might be surprised by the bond that could form. It's up to you. You tell me what you're willing and able to do, and we'll work from there."

Were they negotiating her limits? She'd never once had this conversation with a man. She'd come to believe limit negotiations were a myth. She'd tried to bring it up in her first kink relationship, but the guy had scoffed at her and assured her that he would *just know* if he was going too far.

Well, he *had* just known, and then he'd crossed all her lines anyway. And the one after him. And the one after him. And finally Jason. They'd all done it. After the first guy, she hadn't brought up negotiations and limits because she was afraid they'd start in on some "slaves don't get to negotiate" bullshit.

She knew some people somewhere negotiated. It was the codified rule of things on the surface. And she knew some girls who claimed they had, and that their dominants had honored their boundaries. But snakes lurking in the wood pile were all too common in a lifestyle where it was hard to tell real abuse from pretend by just looking.

"Mina . . . did I lose you?" Lindsay urged her back to the present. "Yes or no on intercourse? I need you to be one hundred percent honest with me, or this won't work."

"I mean, I *can* do intercourse. It's not like I'm broken." But wasn't she?

"I'm marking, *no*. This isn't about what you can try to cope with without becoming catatonic. We're talking ideal situations. Let me see what I can find for you. At that point we can decide if any concessions need to be made."

Of course concessions would be made. Why was he pretending to give her the option to opt out of the one sexual act that even vanilla society had deemed mandatory or it wasn't *real sex*?

This wasn't going to happen. She didn't trust that Lindsay had the power to stop her from being hurt by whatever random pervert he hooked her up with. And she didn't buy that he had access to such a man in the first place.

She took a deep breath and laid out clearly and succinctly what she wanted. "No penetration. No physical pain. Everything else is okay." She was sure any theoretical master would ask what else could there possibly be if all of that was off the table?

She expected Lindsay to laugh at her. These things didn't exist. Anywhere. Maybe if she built a robot, she could program him to her exact weird specifications.

"Okay. Are you serious about this? If I find someone who meets these needs for you, will you do it?"

Mina waited for the punchline, but it didn't seem to be coming.

"I'm asking for impossible things, and . . . I've got these scars. Even if you could find some completely bizarre man who would go along with all of this, he wouldn't want me once he saw the scars." And he probably wouldn't be able to deal with the drama of her emotional scars, either.

"May I see them?" Lindsay asked.

"I-I'd have to take off my shirt."

He raised a brow and leaned back in his seat. It was a challenge. It was a dare. And a small part of her buzzed with excitement, because it was also a show. God, what the fuck was wrong with her? Even now, after everything, she was so fucked in the head.

Mina stood and turned around. She unbuttoned the silk top and let it slide off her shoulders. She'd never shown anyone her scars in full light—at least not anyone who wasn't beating or fucking her. She'd worried that if things progressed with Tony, she'd have to insist on sex with the lights off.

He'd think she was a prude or insecure, but it would be better than him seeing what had been done to her and maybe getting sadistic ideas of his own.

Circular marks from cigarettes ran down the backs of her arms and her legs. There were whip scars and knife scars on her back. Most of it had healed enough that she didn't look like a total monster, but the scars were definitely distracting. Mina couldn't imagine how they wouldn't be.

She jumped when a warm finger traced one of them.

A whimper left her throat.

"Yes, you definitely need a proper master. I don't think this will be a problem. You'd be surprised the number of men who have a hero complex and wouldn't mind at all. You can put your shirt back on."

Mina's fingers shook as she struggled to get the buttons back in their holes. When she sat, the doctor pressed a cup of tea into her hands.

"It's camomile. It'll soothe you."

She took a sip and gathered the courage to say what she'd wanted to say since she'd stepped into his office. "Do you have somebody? A pet or slave or sub or whatever?"

Lindsay shook his head. "Between my work here and . . . my other work . . . I don't feel I have the time or energy to devote to someone like that."

"Oh."

He was letting her down easy.

She stared into the cup, trying not to notice as he moved closer to her and leaned against the desk, his leg a mere inches from hers. All one of them would have to do is shift the barest amount to be touching the other.

She flinched when his hand brushed her cheek.

"Mina, look at me."

She looked up, wishing she could bury all the vulner-ability she'd allowed this man to see, wishing he wanted her because if there was a single person on the planet who could give her faith that this could work and that she could be happy, it was Lindsay.

"It's not that I'm not attracted. I really don't have time. I can't give you what you need outside this office."

She nodded and took another sip of tea to distract herself from his looming closeness.

Dr. Smith moved back behind the desk. "I'm going to call an associate of mine tomorrow to see if he'll meet with you and if he thinks we should accept you into the program. I will warn you that he will touch you, and not in a safe, platonic way."

Mina felt the tremble coming back into her hands and set the teacup down on the desk.

Lindsay pretended not to notice. "He will touch you. He will look at you. But he will not cause you pain, and he will not penetrate you. Do you trust me?"

"Y-yes." She shouldn't. She shouldn't trust any other perverts after what had happened with the last four. But the doctor felt more solid, more stable somehow.

"If he agrees to the meeting will you go and do whatever he asks within those parameters?"

"Y-yes."

He nodded and scribbled something down in the notebook. "Very well."

"A-are we finished here?"

Lindsay glanced at the clock. "Unless you have more to talk about. Do you want me to prescribe a sedative?"

"No." There wasn't a pill in the world that would let her sleep tonight. She gathered her purse and started for the door.

"Mina?"

She turned to find intense eyes on her once again.

"Whether or not you end up in our program, you will not speak of this conversation to anyone. I care a great deal about you and your well-being. It would make me extraordinarily unhappy to have to hurt you. Do we understand each other?"

"I-I don't know anything."

"You suspect. That's enough. I can't let you leave this office unless we understand each other, because if you open your mouth to anyone, no one will ever find you. And that would pain me."

Every man she trusted turned out to be a monster.

For three days, Mina convinced herself that her late Sunday night meeting with Dr. Smith had been a dream, that it had never happened at all. She'd been too tired. It had been too late. And it had been too weird. There was no way any of that had happened. It was just her sexual fantasies and fears crossing wires and spitting out a fucked-up dream.

But then her cell phone rang. The doctor's number flashed across the screen.

"Hello?"

"Anton will meet with you. Remember, dear Mina, this is only an interview. No promises."

She still didn't know what the *program* was. She'd been too stunned to ask many questions the previous night, and she had a feeling that too many questions would only put her in more danger.

"Mina?" Lindsay said. "Are you still willing to do this?"

"I-I don't know what I'm agreeing to. You're scaring me."

He sighed. "You aren't agreeing to anything just yet except to go see Anton and obey him for one afternoon. You will enjoy yourself. No harm will come to you. Afterward, he and I will speak and make a decision. You aren't committing yourself to anything long term at this point. Can I tell Anton to expect you at four o'clock today?"

"I'm supposed to work this evening."

"There are other waitressing jobs if this doesn't pan out. In fact, I'll find you a better job personally. Forget the restaurant. Go."

There might be other restaurants, but the one that employed her was fancy enough that the tips kept her rent paid. She doubted Lindsay could find her something better.

Mina closed her eyes. "Yes. I'll be there at four." The *yes* bounced and echoed inside her brain so loud she barely heard the directions to Anton's office. A place called *Dome*.

"Wait, isn't that a spa?" Mina asked, bewildered.

"Like I said, you'll enjoy yourself. I'm told Anton is very good at what he does."

The line went dead before she could reply. She stared at the phone, wondering if she should call him back, but it felt inappropriate. This whole thing was inappropriate.

She spent the next three hours trying to convince herself that she wasn't going to show up, but it rang false even in her own mind. Besides, she worried if she didn't show up that Lindsay would think she was talking to the police or something. She had no doubt his earlier threat had implied her untimely death—not that he'd keep her prisoner somewhere.

She tried, unsuccessfully to not think about Lindsay Smith keeping her prisoner somewhere. Because for all the wrong it was, the idea made her stomach flutter.

Five minutes until four, Mina stared up at *Dome*. The building looked like a giant soap bubble, with the front looking as if it had been dipped in bronze. The doors were a shiny reflective glass.

Mina stared at her reflection as she approached the building. She looked so mousy standing there all insecure in jeans and a t-shirt. Should she have dressed more sexy? Maybe she should have dressed like she did to see the therapist. Anton wouldn't be impressed with this look. And maybe that was the point. She could still tact-fully extricate herself from all of this if the answer was "No." She'd have to find another therapist. After this she wasn't sure she could look Lindsay in the face again—particularly not when she'd practically begged him to dominate her.

A silver bell overhead jingled as she opened the heavy door. She tried not to appear self-conscious and out of place as she approached the reception desk. "I have an appointment with Anton?" It should have been a statement, but out of Mina's mouth it became a question.

The blonde behind the counter smiled brightly as she scanned their appointment system. "Four o'clock. Right on time, Ms. Calloway. Just have a seat, and Anton will be right with you."

The blonde pressed a button on the desk phone and said, "Your four o'clock is here."

Mina sat on a sofa next to a large palm plant. Minutes later, a door opened and out stepped one of the most attractive men Mina had ever laid eyes on. She'd thought Lindsay was something, but this guy . . . The idea of obeying him for the afternoon was beginning to sound appealing—as long as he didn't hurt her.

Anton was much younger than Lindsay, by a decade at least. He had longish wavy dark hair that fell over chiseled cheekbones. He looked like he lived at the gym, which made it a great mystery how he'd found time in his schedule to be here today at all.

"Mina Calloway, yes?" he said. His accent sounded Russian, maybe Ukrainian. She could never tell the difference between the dialects. The accent made him seem even more dangerous, but he was so attractive that it would be nearly impossible to see him and run in the other direction.

"Y-yes." Her feet, without her awareness or direction, somehow moved her from the sofa to Anton's side.

"Janette, this is my last appointment for the day. You can pack your things and go home now," he said, his wolfish gaze not leaving Mina.

"Y-yes, sir," the blonde said from the reception area.

At least Mina wasn't the only one here who couldn't manage to speak without her voice wavering. There was some small comfort in that.

Anton took her hand in his and kissed the back of it. His fingers were long, strong.

"W-what is it exactly that you do here?" she asked.

He laughed. "You are adorable. I like you."

He took her to a massage room with candles, a burbling fountain, and eastern ambient music. On one wall, a screen showed images from the spa as a soothing voice explained the spa's philosophies and services.

The screen went black, and the deadbolt clicked. When she turned, Anton blocked the door. Okay that wasn't ominous or anything.

Her mental sarcasm stopped short as she gripped the side of the massage table and doubled over, her breath coming hard and fast as the panic swamped her. This wasn't a good time for this.

Lindsay said he wouldn't hurt you. The voice of reason tried to push through her anxiety, but it didn't matter what the doctor promised. It didn't even matter if he was sincere or truly believed she'd be safe. Right now, it was just her and a complete stranger locked in this little room—probably alone in the building now. He could do any fucked-up thing he wanted, and there was nothing Mina could do to stop him.

Strong arms gripped her and pulled her to stand. "I've got you," he said.

Why this should be comforting, she didn't know, but she did feel comforted all the same by the apparent concern in his voice.

"Come with me." He led her through a second door to a small attached apartment.

"D-do you live here?" Mina asked, trying to keep things light, trying to forget she was locked in with this guy.

"No, but it's a long drive to my home, and I've been known to sleep here on occasion. I own *Dome.*"

He took a bottle of wine and glasses out of a cabinet in the kitchenette. "Here," he said, when he'd poured the wine. "Drink. It will settle you."

If she hadn't watched him open a brand new bottle and pour it in front of her, she might have been too paranoid to accept the drink, but the only thing in it was wine. It was a brand she recognized and one she liked. She downed it in one long swallow, not caring what Anton would think of her slamming the wine back like a refugee from a 12-step program.

Within minutes, the warm, tingly buzz crept over her face, and she didn't feel like the world was ending—even though it still might be. That would depend on what Anton did to her.

She handed the glass back to him.

"Another?" he asked.

"No." She was afraid to be too drunk with him, afraid to pass out locked away in his secret apartment.

He put the glass in the sink and sat beside her. She was surprised when he pulled her close. Without conscious thought, she leaned against his chest while his fingers caressed her hair and up and down her arm. Even after everything, she drank up the promise and hope of kindness.

"Lindsay explained what we do, didn't he?"

"Well, not exactly. A bit. He was vague." She found herself relaxing as his hand moved to knead the back of her neck.

"And you understand you will be naked and being touched by me in a few moments, yes?"

Maybe she should have taken the second drink. For all her experience in the kink scene, this man left her unbalanced.

She nodded.

Mina sat mute as he undressed her. The lighting was low, and for a moment she thought he might not get a good look at her back, but he moved to the wall and flicked a switch, bathing the room in bright cruel fluorescence.

"Turn," he said, rotating a finger in the air.

She turned away and held her breath. The only sound in the room was the central heat clicking on. Anton made no comment. He didn't trace any of her scars with his fingertips as the doctor had done.

For those moments of silence, Mina found herself more terrified he would reject her than anything else he might do. Her damage was too much on display. It made her a freak. The longer this silence dragged, the more the images of Jason and the others flashed through her mind. The laughing, the taunts, the humiliation, the pain.

Why had she allowed any of that?

Why was she here now?

"In this room, you will call me, Sir."

"Yes, Sir."

Something familiar. This would be okay. Even if he were a terrible person like the others, no one else had started hurting her the first day . . . they'd all pretended at first. He'd probably pretend, too. Then she would go home and forget all this.

He perched on the edge of the bed. "Crawl to me. I want to watch how you move."

She went to her hands and knees and moved across the thick carpet.

"Stay on your knees and spread your legs." That accent touched places inside her that she'd been sure were gone now. "Sit up straight."

Being under Anton's gaze was the very definition of scrutiny. Before it had been scenes at play parties followed by scenes that flowed into relationships in private . . . kink that flowed into abuse.

Here, Anton held a quiet power, like the doctor's in some ways. Different in others. These men were a whole other level—a level she'd been unaware existed. She was afraid to know more. The past chased her, biting at her heels, telling her to run. But all she could do was obey him.

Anton leaned forward. "That's a good girl," he cooed as his hand moved between her legs. "So wet. Does it not embarrass you to be this excited kneeling at my feet?"

"No, Sir."

"You're very brave to be here."

She tensed at that, even as his fingers caressed the bundle of nerves between her thighs.

"Relax. That was not a threat. Just an observation." He stroked the side of her throat, leaving behind a trail of the evidence of her excitement.

Anton's hands strayed to her breasts, the lightest touch causing her nipples to harden.

"I've seen enough. You can get dressed now. Lindsay will call you in a few days if we are interested in you."

"Yes, Sir."

He opened the door and disappeared into the depths of the spa.

What had just happened? She wanted to run after him and ask if she'd done something wrong. But she knew the problem. Anton was repulsed by the scars.

She hurriedly dressed, grabbed her bag, and slipped out of the building. It had already started to get dark, and she was grateful not to have the garish bright sun shining down on her to illuminate her shame.

Mina sat behind the wheel of her car in stunned silence until the cold air seeped in through the edges of the windows.

She felt used. Of course they weren't going to call her. Anton had probably taken one look at the wreck that was her back and decided that her face couldn't make up for it, that there was nothing she could do to impress or please enough to erase it.

When she reached her apartment, she poured a glass of wine and went straight to her room and stripped. She held the glass in one hand and a cigarette in the other as she craned to study her reflection in the full-length mirror. She'd tried to pretend it wasn't that bad. But it *was* that bad—even in the low lighting she kept in her room to minimize it. What had it been like in the bright light she'd been subjected to with Anton?

Even without the dreams and panic attacks, it wouldn't have worked with Tony because eventually he would have seen them. And how could she explain? Only a sadist could love those scars, and a sadist would only add to them.

Mina brushed away a tear. She hadn't realized she'd started crying again. Maybe she should lay off the wine. It made her more self-pitying.

It felt as if the Russian's hand lingered between her legs, those brief caresses that made her believe for the smallest second that something good could happen to her . . . a gentle dominance that wouldn't turn to violence. She'd expected something more would happen. She'd found herself oddly hoping for it, praying she could handle it and finally find what she'd been searching for. But they didn't want her.

She'd gone for the interview, and now it was over. She'd find another therapist and move on.

Mina nearly broke her neck getting out of the shower to answer the phone. Dr. Smith's number flashed on her screen.

"You missed your appointment Monday. Are you sick?"

"No, I'm fine," she said.

"Why weren't you here?"

The way he said it made her feel as if she'd done something horrifically wrong, something that called for punishment. The latter thought made her cringe.

"I just thought that under the circumstances, maybe I should find another doctor."

There was a long silence on the other end of the phone. "What circumstances would those be? I'm confused." He didn't sound confused.

Now it was her turn to be silent because she couldn't give voice to the rejection.

"By the way," he said, "Anton and I finally had a chance to speak. I was going to tell you yesterday, but you decided not to show up. I considered not contacting you at all, but I've had time to calm down. Meet me at the office."

"Now?" she squeaked.

"No, next year. Of course, now. Right now. I expect you sitting across from me in thirty minutes or I will be extremely disappointed."

"B-but it's eleven at night." She'd been about ready to put on her pajamas and eat some cookie dough ice cream. These were big plans for a Thursday night.

"Thirty minutes."

The line went dead. She stared at the phone wondering what would happen if she didn't show up. He had her address in his files. Would he send goons to her apartment? Would he come himself? Was he feeling antsy that she might talk to the cops about him?

She still wasn't sure what she could say even if she wanted to report him. What was she reporting him for, exactly? He'd been just vague enough that anything she said was going to sound stupid. They'd probably laugh her out of the station or charge her with something for wasting their time. She could report Anton, but for what? She hadn't paid him. Weren't massage therapists allowed to have consensual sexual interactions with people who weren't paying them? Like everybody else? Besides, nothing of note had happened.

What if they'd rejected her but now the doctor felt skittish about what little non-information she had about his vague but possibly illegal activities?

As she entertained these possibilities, she bypassed her pajamas for a pair of jeans and a T-shirt. She didn't bother with anything nice. She was sure being late would be worse than the horror of him seeing her in ratty jeans.

Thirty minutes later, she sat exactly where he'd told her to be, feeling like a teenager in the principal's office. She hadn't realized until now that her nice blouses and pencil skirts and heels and red lipstick had been her armor. It made her feel powerful and strong enough to exist in the same space with him for an hour at a time.

That power had been traded for a pony tail and scuffed tennis shoes.

"Laundry day?" Lindsay asked from his side of the desk.

"It's eleven-thirty."

"Yes. You made it. I had considered not making the offer since you so rudely missed our appointment yesterday, but Anton and I spoke and he believes we can place you with a proper master if you are still interested in pursuing this."

She hadn't expected that. "I-I don't know if I can do it."

"Fine. Leave. Hide away in your cocoon. Avoid men. Avoid relationships. Avoid yourself. What do I care?"

Here it was: the moment when he turned on her to reveal the beast behind the civilized facade. She cringed and braced herself, ready to throw her arms up in a lame and ineffective self-defense pose if necessary.

She hadn't realized she'd squeezed her eyes shut until his warm hands were on her arms.

"You're clenching the leather. It was just reupholstered," he said, disengaging her fingernails from the arm rest. "I know you're scared, and I'm not helping. The truth is, I have a lot to lose, too. I let you leave my presence after giving you enough rope to possibly hang me with. It was foolish. And now the only thing that can make any of this okay for everyone is if you'll just take that one small step. Just trust me one more time to get you from point A to B. You will be happy at the end of this process if you'll just trust me."

He was as good as admitting to being a criminal. Why should she trust a criminal?

"Did Anton hurt you?" he asked.

"No." She desperately wanted to call him *Sir*. In spite of all the things she'd been through, there was a peace in that title. In any title. At least until they turned on her.

"Anton said you were very excited. Very responsive."

She was always excited in the beginning when things were new and the mask of kindness was still in place.

"If I agreed to be matched with someone, how do I know I would be safe? What if he only seemed okay, and then he started hurting me later?"

Lindsay returned to his side of the desk. "We routinely check in with our girls. Early on, it's once a week, then once a month, then every few months. When we're sure everything is fine, it's a yearly video call. Whoever buys you will have a contract with us. The contract may not be enforceable by law, but they know the consequences of breaking it. We will *handle* anyone foolish enough to break our contract and get the girl out of there. We don't have to do it often because we screen carefully."

"What if he threatens me, and I say everything is okay because I'm scared of him?"

"We visit in person. Not me, but it will be someone who is fully capable of handling any issue that may arise. We will remove you from a bad situation."

Mina's brain finally caught up with part of what the doctor said. It wasn't as if she hadn't suspected as much, but to hear it was another thing. "Buy? Someone would be *buying* me?"

"Yes. Do you think we do this out of some charitable urge?"

"Would I be seeing any of this money?"

"Not a penny."

"What if I say no?"

Lindsay's face appeared smooth and unrippled, mild and untroubled. But his fingers gripped his own newly reupholstered leather. "Then you can go home." His voice was tight.

"Would you still see me as a patient?"

He relaxed a fraction. "If you wish."

Of course, because then he could keep tabs on her and know if she could still be trusted. He'd know the moment she had an urge to fill out a police report.

She wanted to know if he'd been this open with other prospects. Somehow she doubted it, and she was afraid to make him any more skittish.

"Mina? I've risked myself and my safety because I care about you. I care that you are happy and safe and protected, and that your life works out for you in all the ways you've ever dreamed without the ugly things that have cast a shadow over you. You've been coming here for a while now. You obviously feel safe enough to be alone with me. If you can just place your trust in me a little further, I can give you everything you've ever wanted. I promise you."

She'd be lying if she said his impassioned speech had no effect. Whether her instincts were right or wrong on this, she did trust him. And if anyone could ensure no one ever hurt her again, she trusted Lindsay could. He radiated a confident power that she'd yet to encounter. If there was such a thing, he was the real deal.

And if he was the real deal, then he knew where to find more of his kind.

"What would happen if I said yes?"

"If you agree, you will go home tonight and pack your bags. Pack anything you have any strong attachment to because you won't be returning. A car will pick you up and take you to an estate where you will be trained, and a match will be found for you. At that point, once we've screened him properly and he's signed all our paperwork and paid for you, you will be turned over to his care."

No. This is madness. Unless you have an absolute death wish, this is not the way.

But the place inside her that Jason hadn't yet killed—the place Anton had briefly touched—cried out for the hope that the kind of master Lindsay described could be real and that somehow this mystery man could undo everything those before him had done. She'd been barely existing since Jason. As fucked up and horrible as it was with him, as uncertain and abusive . . . she didn't know how to be normal anymore.

"I live at the estate," Lindsay continued, oblivious to her inner struggle. "As does Anton. You will meet other girls. No one will do anything we talked about in your limits, or they will face consequences."

"Why do you do this?"

"Find a need and fill it. Business 101. Do we have a deal, Mina?" The devil smiled at her as the devil does when he's about to take your soul in a pact signed with blood.

"I . . ." She wanted to say yes. As insane as it was she wanted to believe this wasn't the worst thing she could agree to.

"Go home and pack your things. A car will be by for you at seven in the evening. Get into the car and start a new life. Or don't. I'll instruct the driver to leave at seven-thirty with or without you."

Two

Mina paced the apartment. She'd packed her luggage: clothes, toiletries, and a few items of sentimental value that she couldn't part with—mostly old photos and an ornate silver ring with small black stones that her grandmother had given her before she'd passed away.

She still remembered her grandmother taking the ring off and placing it in her hand. "I'm not long for this world, Caramina. Take it so the others don't fight over it. The silver will ward evil away from you. If the ring ever burns you, you know you're in the company of someone or something bad, and you must get away from it."

Mina had known the delirium was setting in, that her grandmother was talking nonsense, confusing dreams with reality. Still, she liked to believe the ring truly did have powers and could protect her.

"Did it ever burn you?" she'd asked, playing along.

"Only once. I shot that motherfucker in the face."

Mina had nodded and pretended to believe her. The woman hadn't even owned a gun, and she certainly had never shot anyone in the face or anywhere else.

After her grandmother died, Mina had sorted through the bottom drawers in the old woman's closet to find the box that went with the ring. There it had stayed for the past three years. It hurt her to look at it.

There had been a fight about the ring. Three different cousins believed it should have been theirs. Soon after, Mina had drifted away from the family and moved into another city where she'd been ever since. Her grandmother had been the only one tethering her to the people who were supposed to be her blood.

The ring story was nonsense, but she wanted to believe that if she'd been wearing it when she'd met Jason, she would have known he was bad and stayed away.

So much pain and permanent scarring could have been avoided if she'd known he was a flame to stay well enough away from.

She slipped the ring on her finger as the clock on the mantle chimed out seven ominously hollow gongs. Outside, a black sedan with tinted windows pulled to the curb. The driver didn't honk. He just sat with the engine idling. Waiting for her.

Mina went through the apartment searching for anything else she might miss if she never saw it again. When she looked at the clock again, it was seven-twenty. The sedan still idled. Her heart palpitated wildly, trying to escape her chest.

She'd packed as Lindsay requested, but the packing had felt more like something to pass time. Once the driver left, she'd have plenty of time to unpack and put her things back where they belonged. She wasn't going. She'd known she wasn't going from the moment she'd taken the suitcases out of the closet.

She'd just wanted the option. If she wasn't packed, she wouldn't have the option because there was no way she could leave absolutely everything behind to go . . . wherever the hell she was being taken. But to admit that to herself and not pack at all was to admit she would never have love again. If someone didn't arrange something safe for her, only loneliness stretched before her.

Her tenth cigarette of the evening shook between her fingers. Would they let her smoke? Would her master let her smoke? Would they make her quit? A lot of people thought smoking was a disgusting habit. She agreed, but it calmed her nerves. It made her feel like she could hold things together even while they were falling apart around her.

What if they wouldn't let her smoke?

She laughed in the stillness of the apartment. She wasn't going. Her smoking habit was safe.

At seven twenty-five, she went to the window again. Her stomach knotted tighter with each minute that passed. She should make some dinner. But she couldn't. She had to watch the sedan drive away.

At seven-thirty, right on schedule, the car began to pull slowly from the curb. A panic burst out of Mina's chest, and she ran out the door and down the single flight of stairs. Thank God she was only on the second floor. Outside, she grabbed a rock, ran down the road, and threw it at the car. It hit the back window, and the brake lights came on.

Mina dropped the cigarette she'd been holding and put it out with her shoe.

A perturbed man stepped out of the car and glared at her.

"You were supposed to pick me up," she said, suddenly flustered and wanting to run again.

"I waited half an hour as instructed. If you couldn't be ready by that time . . ."

"Can you please help me with my bags?" Had she just said that?

The driver gave a curt nod. He pulled the car to the front of the building and went inside to get her things.

The drive was silent and long—most of it outside the city in the countryside. It was late when they pulled up to what could only be described as a mansion. And even that didn't do it justice. Maybe castle? How did this place exist? How did no one know about it?

The estate seemed to be in the middle of a forest. Had they blocked satellites, somehow? Surely if this place existed, someone would have seen it and reported on it. People would want to know what it was, who owned it, why it was out in the middle of nowhere.

The driver was buzzed in through an iron gate, and they drove up a large hill to the house. The sedan pulled into an expansive circular driveway.

"Go in. Your luggage will be brought to your room," the driver said when the car stopped.

She trudged up the stairs like a child trying to get out of going to school. Before she could pull the old-fashioned doorbell, the door opened.

"Mina, you made it." Lindsay took both of her hands and pulled her into the sprawling estate. "I wasn't sure you'd come."

"I almost didn't. I cracked the back window of your car with a rock." Better for her to tell him than the driver.

Lindsay raised an eyebrow. "I see. Let me show you to your suite."

Mina gaped at the marble floors and ornate staircase in the entry hall. She couldn't believe she was staying here. The doctor let go of one of her hands, but kept a grasp on the other as he led her to the staircase.

A man with dark black hair and eyes even darker approached. "Lindsay, I need to meet with you privately."

"I'll be with you in a few minutes. My office," Lindsay responded.

"Fine."

Mina shrank and hid behind the doctor as the stranger stared, his gaze panning over her. She was grateful she wasn't wearing anything sexy—just frumpy jeans and a t-shirt. The way he looked at her was bad enough, but if she'd looked remotely decent, it would have been worse.

Suddenly her whole body burned. She looked down at the ring, her eyes going wide. Was the ring . . .? Of course not! That was insane! She'd loved her grandmother, but her delirious ramblings days before her death hadn't been exactly factual or trustworthy. Other tales of hers had included wanting to take a canoeing vacation on the moon, and the insistence that her canoe be pink so the aliens wouldn't take it.

The heat was just the beginning of a panic attack. The feeling went away by the time they reached the top of the stairs, though she'd looked behind her to make sure the stranger wasn't following. She hoped her door had a big, heavy lock on it.

They went to the end of the hallway and up another, less opulent flight of stairs. "The only room we have left right now is a tower. I'm afraid it's quite a trek. And our elevator is out at the moment."

They had an elevator? Of course there was an elevator. This place looked like a gothic-themed dungeon resort. Give kinksters unlimited funds to create any place they wanted, and this would be the obvious end result.

They ascended several more flights. At each floor was a long hallway and several rooms. There was no hallway at the top of the last staircase, just a landing and a large door with wood and ironwork. Lindsay unlocked it and urged her inside.

The room was clean and large and circular. The walls were stone with small windows going all the way around. A bathroom was built into the tower, breaking the perfect circle. But the bathroom walls were glass.

"A curtain pulls around it—not that you'll need it," he said. "We have a cafeteria you can visit during certain hours to eat. And there is a game room and a pool. We recently enclosed the pool in glass so it can be used year round more easily. Plenty to amuse yourself with."

The tower might be creepy, but the view of the grounds from this high up was amazing—even at night.

The room had a flat screen television mounted on the wall and a king-sized bed covered by a simple black duvet. Chains were bolted into the wall. There was a large trunk at the foot of the bed which Mina assumed probably contained BDSM-related things. A chest of drawers stood near the bed.

The room also had a writing desk with a plush purple chair in front of it. A black binder sat on the desk next to an old-fashioned rotary phone. She hadn't seen one of those since she was a child at her grandmother's house.

"It's decorative." He pointed to a gray box on the wall. "We recently extended our intercom system to all suites. We have a few phones with outside lines, but you can understand why those are not for your use. If you need something, use the intercom. The rules of how you are to comport yourself while here are in the binder. Read and follow them. Are you hungry?"

She *was* hungry. She hadn't realized they were going to be driving so long or arrive so late. Maybe she should have made dinner at a normal time, but she'd been too nervous to eat until her fate was decided.

"The kitchen closed half an hour ago, but I'll send something up."

"T-thank you."

Lindsay took both of her hands into his again. "You are going to be fine, Mina. I promise we will handle you with care, and I'll find you someone who won't hurt you."

He pulled a silver bracelet from his pocket. "Have you ever been under house arrest?" He tried to make it sound like a joke.

Mina shook her head.

"I won't lock you in your room, but you have to stay on the grounds—for obvious reasons."

He may as well have gone ahead and said, "You've seen too much already to be set free." But he simply locked the metal band around her wrist.

"It'll zap you if you go outside the property lines, so keep that in mind if you venture outside. If it beeps, you are to stop whatever you're doing and come to my office on the first floor. Someone can guide you to it. I need to go meet with Brian now."

Lindsay left her, and she sat on the edge of the bed. She prayed she wouldn't have to interact with Brian. He was exactly the kind of man she'd been trying to escape.

Brian impatiently paced Lindsay's office, distracted by thoughts of the new girl. She'd been so exotic. Dark olive skin and silky raven hair that went halfway down her back. Her eyes were a luminous green, which made them seem to glow against the dark palette of her skin—like a cat staring out at him from the shadows.

She was scared of him. Smart girl. Everyone was scared of him. If he were being completely honest, sometimes he scared himself.

Brian considered himself a monster with a purpose. His job at the house was to mete out the more sadistic punishments that the other trainers didn't have the stomach for—and especially to train the girls who were at the extreme level of masochistic and too much for the others to handle. At the end of the day most of the trainers were lightweights living out their soft-core porn fantasies for a healthy paycheck.

He got all the grunt work, but he wasn't complaining. It fed the dark, swirling shadow that crawled underneath his skin demanding blood and retribution. If he went too long without feeding it, his skin started to burn and itch. And he'd get headaches. The shrink said it was all psychosomatic. All in his head. No, only the headaches were in his head. The other issues were more all encompassing.

Each trainer was a type of tool in the grand scheme of their ambitious enterprise. Brian was a blunt force instrument designed to do damage, create fear, and keep every girl obedient on threat of being sent to him. He was the enforcer. With him there, the house only needed one.

When he was hurting someone, his own demons stopped tormenting him briefly. The images and flashbacks from his youth short-circuited, and the loop stopped playing for those few moments while he made memories that would give his victim flashbacks of her own. It was an ugly form of transference, but it let him sleep at night, however unsoundly.

Before they'd started this unusual and very illegal business venture, Lindsay had tried to put him on medication. But the drugs just made him foggy on top of everything else. Acting out his sadism on living flesh was the only drug that worked.

In fact, one might say that the house revolved in some sense around Brian. He was the seed that had sprouted into this deliciously wicked idea. To the casual observer, Anton ran the show, with Lindsay and Gabe right behind him in the pecking order. Most of the myriad trainers in the house deferred to them. But the three of them, plus Brian, were all partners—equal now that they'd all invested into the business. Brian was a silent partner. He'd gone along with the outward ruse of being a mere *employee* for optics.

God forbid the people they do business with think the sadist in the dungeon was an equal partner. By definition weren't they all sociopaths to be doing this? Brian was the only one who was honest about it. The others wanted to believe they were good.

And what of the buyers? No one was a spotless lamb, here. No sense pretending about it.

He was startled when Lindsay entered the office—all business. Brian began to speak, but the doctor raised a hand and picked up the phone from his desk.

"Could you prepare some food for our newest guest? She's in the south tower. Yes, thank you."

Lindsay disconnected the call and settled in the high-backed leather chair. "What is it, Brian?"

"Who's the new girl?" His attempt at nonchalance was weak. The last time he showed an interest in a new girl Anton had forbidden him from going near her. Too much eagerness would just start a fight he didn't want to deal with.

"The new girl is Mina. She won't be your concern. You will not be training her."

Brian slumped in a chair on the other side of the desk. "Is that right? Is this a new trend? The house protecting everyone from me? First Vivian, now Mina? Is she Michael's, too?"

Michael had gone to college with most of them and had been asked to join their endeavor but considered the whole business distasteful. That is until he suspected his wife had a touch of the kink and wanted them to train her for his pleasure. Well, all of them except for Brian who'd been banned from the fun and games.

Lindsay looked annoyed. "No, she isn't Michael's." He opened his briefcase and slid typed papers across the desk. There were several, held together by a thin green paper clip. "This is the contract her eventual buyer will sign. I made promises to her which I intend to keep."

Brian scanned the document, raising a brow at some of the stipulations. "This is unusual, these kinds of boundaries." It wasn't unheard of to allow a girl to set some ground rules—if she'd earned the right—but these ground rules were atypical to say the least.

The doctor shrugged. "We've dealt with unusual before. I believe I can help her find someone appropriate who won't damage her further. You can see why your particular brand of sadism isn't going to work in this situation. From my talks with her, I think she needs very little training. It's not as if non-sadistic masters are impossible to find. The no-penetration rule may be a harder match, but I was thinking if we found someone who has another girl or two from us, so he wouldn't explicitly need Mina in that way . . . and we trusted him . . . Repeat buyers aren't unheard of."

Brian slid the papers back across the desk. "Good luck with that." Lindsay got far too close to his patients—especially the ones he brought to the house. The doctor's unhealthy interest in this girl would bring nothing but chaos. It was a bad business decision. Those boundaries meant she wouldn't go for much at auction, which meant she was hardly worth the cost of training and housing.

"What was it you wanted?" Lindsay asked, distracted.

"I wanted to inform you that I'm taking tomorrow off. I've got some errands to run in the city and need to get out. I haven't had a day off in six months."

"All right. We can do without you for a day."

"Thanks, Doc."

"Brian? Are you sleeping?"

He shrugged. How many times was Lindsay going to harp on his sleep patterns? They'd batted this issue back and forth for years now.

"I can prescribe you a sedative."

"No drugs. I'm not doing that shit again. It fucks me up." *Worse.*

"Just a mild tranquilizer. It wouldn't have the same side effects."

No, they'd be different and new and exciting side effects.

"No," Brian practically growled.

The doctor held his hands up in surrender. "Fine. But you need more sleep. You're getting run down."

"Give me someone to punish. I'll sleep like a fucking baby. Otherwise, stay out of it."

Brian stopped by the kitchen when he left the doctor. A tray had been prepared with covered leftovers and a glass of water.

"I'll take it up to our guest. Thanks, Phyllis."

She cringed but nodded.

He wasn't sure what compelled him to take Mina's tray up, but he wanted to see her close up and alone. He wanted to smell her shampoo again. He wanted to breathe in the scent of her fear when there was nobody there to protect her from him. If Lindsay kept too strict an eye on things, this might be his only opportunity before she slipped through his fingers entirely.

When he reached the tower, he knocked with three sharp raps.

"Just a minute," came a soft reply.

When she opened the door, her face was scrubbed of make-up. She wore casual pajamas—the kind popular both with college freshmen and old ladies. Her feet were bare except for some glittery purple polish. When she looked up to see his face, she took several steps back.

Brian stepped into the room and set the tray on the desk. "Mina, I brought your dinner."

"T-thank you." She was still backing up.

He wasn't sure if she was aware of her continued retreat. She took another step back and tripped over her suitcase. Brian didn't know why, but he rushed to help. In her fall, her shirt rode up, displaying vicious scars. They were on her back and wrapped around to her side.

He couldn't resist the urge to run his hand over one of the puckered marks.

For a moment time stopped. She froze as he lingered over the scar that was visible to him, his fingertip caress-ing back and forth.

Mina seemed to snap out of it and jerked away. She struggled to pull the shirt back down as he helped her stand. He'd wanted to scare her. The predatory instinct had awakened to her fear downstairs. And yet, now . . . Brian couldn't articulate how he felt, even in his own mind. He couldn't remember a single time he'd helped one of the girls if they'd fallen or gotten hurt. He was more likely to laugh or to use it as an excuse to punish them for their clumsiness. But his protective reaction to Mina's tumble had been instantaneous and instinctive.

She watched him with those wide, frightened green eyes, her arms crossed over her chest in a defensive pose.

He didn't speak another word. He'd wanted to intimidate her, threaten her, revel with sadistic glee in her fear, but all he could do was turn around and leave. He berated himself as he went down each flight of stairs all the way to the lowest level—to the dungeons. It was physically the farthest he could get from her, but it was also where he lived.

There were a few small dungeon rooms underneath the west wing of the house that the other trainers used, but this set of rooms was all his.

He stomped down the long, dimly lit hallway, past doors to the cells he used to correct bad girls' behavior. At the end of the hallway was the door to his suite. He slammed it behind him and peeled off his shirt.

A full-length antique mirror stood on one end of the room. He turned on a nearby lamp and twisted to look at his back, running his fingers over old scars. A few wrapped around his sides. Just like hers. He and Mina were matching macabre portraits of other people's wrath.

The mirror shattered as Brian's fist connected with it. He sat on the edge of the bed, his head in his bleeding hands, and cried. Sobbed, really. He was thankful he hadn't left any of the girls in the dungeon cells tonight, thankful no one could hear him down here.

A memory pushed itself through one of the normally-locked doors in his mind. He kept seeing it, over and over, his stepmother whipping him with the switch, screaming at him for letting the dog pee on the floor, then locking him under the stairs without dinner. It wasn't as if he could control the old dog's bladder. She'd thrown the terrified dog in as well. Brian had woken the next morning in a pool of the animal's urine with flea bites all over him and wounds that got so infected from the filth he'd been left in that he'd almost died. He'd only been nine that time, but it hadn't been the first beating, nor had it been the last.

He tried to push the images out, tried to remember his mother instead. She'd been so kind. She was taken too early—in a car crash. He remembered her smell, and feeling safe and loved. But what he remembered most about her was the music. She'd played old records of Chopin at night to help him sleep as he fought through the fears small children feel—before he knew the real monster who was coming.

His father remarried too soon—a woman he couldn't see the truth about because of his grief.

As a young child Brian hadn't understood why his father didn't protect him from her. But as he got older, he realized how sick the man had been. He'd been too weak to protect Brian from his stepmother's bitter anger. And once he was gone, things only got worse.

Somehow Brian knew he wouldn't be able to sleep tonight, either. Seeing the marks on Mina had created an opposite reaction than he was used to. Knowing Lindsay, the doctor might say that perhaps it was because he wasn't the one in control of the damage. He'd left marks on women worse than what he'd seen of Mina's, but her marks weren't created by his hands. The girls always came to him as blank canvases to paint his sadism across in splashes of bright red.

Those women were his foul stepmother all over again. Not a fucking mark on her. And every time he punished them, he wrote out his revenge across her back. Killing her once hadn't been enough. In the dungeons he could make her pay over and over, make her scream in pain and beg him for mercy he was no longer capable of giving—mercy he didn't want to give. Mercy was weakness. Just an opportunity for someone to swoop in and find the cracks in your soul to hurt you.

Except Mina . . . she wasn't that perfect unmarked canvas. Mina had arrived already broken, and suddenly, somehow this woman he'd only just met was locked under those stairs with him, huddling in the cold darkness.

Three

Mina only worried about five times that her food might be poisoned. When nothing dramatic happened, she let go of the fear. Besides, Brian wouldn't have put something in it. She'd known the moment she looked into those cold dark eyes that he didn't do stealth pain.

He wanted to be there to watch you suffer. He wanted to deliver it with his own hands.

Though it was late, Mina doubted everyone was asleep. Night was when the perverts played. And yet, as she descended the endless stairs—stairs that seemed to have multiplied since the time of her arrival—everything was quiet.

Small lights along the base of the walls illuminated her way. Off the entryway on the first floor was a hallway and another set of stairs that were nearly hidden. A basement? In a house with the purpose this one served, it was probably dungeons. That thought alone should have sent her scurrying back up to her tower.

But she felt drawn, like young Aurora on her sixteenth birthday, moving steadily toward her doom.

She shook herself out of the brief sense of hypnotism. It felt as if some force outside herself pulled her, but whatever was down there was unlikely to be anything she wanted to see.

Mina was about to go back upstairs, when she heard someone coming down the hall. Heavy, sure footfalls. Brian? She was blocked in. If whoever it was kept moving closer, they'd find her. The stairs were her only option.

She slipped down the winding steps as quietly as she could. Behind the stairs at the bottom was another door. When she pushed it open, the heat almost knocked her over. There was an incinerator inside. She shut the door quickly and stayed hidden, waiting.

Whoever she'd heard didn't venture below ground. She felt so stupid now. She moved from behind the staircase to see the rest of what was kept down here.

A long, narrow corridor stretched before her. The floor was concrete, the walls stone. At equal intervals were doors. Five on each side. Straight ahead at the end was another door, this one larger than the rest.

Each door along the passageway had a window with bars, but the door at the end was solid. Mina peeked into one of the rooms—a dungeon, just as she'd suspected. Terrifying implements hung from hooks on the wall. Poles were bolted into the ceiling and floor, meant to tie people to. Shackles hung from one wall. There was a wooden crate filled to the brim with things she wasn't sure about—most likely more implements of pain. There were spanking horses and Saint Andrew's Crosses.

But this place didn't look like a play dungeon. It wasn't like the BDSM parties she'd been to. It wasn't naughty games with a thin veneer of pretend danger— danger that didn't materialize in public, but only later when she'd given her heart to someone.

Mina squinted at a dark spot on the wall and another on the floor. Jesus, were those blood stains?

The door at the end of the hallway opened, and she froze. It was the stupidest and most useless fear response. She was sure that normal people, upon encountering danger and extreme fear, ran. But Mina's muscles responded by going on lock down. She wasn't sure she was even breathing—as if she could simply be still and silent enough to go undetected until the danger passed.

Brian closed the door behind him, his stare holding her captive. She glanced down to note one of his hands was bandaged. They hadn't been when she'd seem him before.

Move. Move! Run run run!

Her muscles might not want to respond to the danger, but her brain screamed at her, throwing all sorts of logic and common-sense sounding plans at her. Like run. And move. But still, her legs stayed frozen inside blocks of imaginary ice that refused to melt and give her freedom.

"What are you doing down here, Mina?"

While words ran through her mind like a psychotic rat darting down a tunnel, her lips refused to relay any of those words to the man moving closer to her in the confined hallway—which shrank smaller with each long stride he took.

He pressed her against the stone, his hands on either side of her, blocking her in. An unnecessary gesture.

He stared at her for a long time—minutes it seemed— his eyes roving, taking in each thread of the lounge-wear she'd gotten at a clearance sale. It had seemed modest when she'd bought it. Now she felt naked and exposed.

Then he did the oddest thing she'd ever seen a human being do. She'd only seen animals do it on nature shows, or vampires in horror movies. He sniffed her like he wanted to eat her. A moment later, he spun her around and pinned her arms above her head.

She shivered as he lifted the back of her shirt. His fingertips skimmed over her scars—running the length of the long ones, then lightly touching the cigarette burns.

She wanted to say something, anything. She wanted to struggle free of his grasp and run. The person standing with her in the dark dungeon hallway was more animal than man, and if even a man couldn't find it in himself to be decent to her, she surely couldn't trust the one that sent all her warning bells ringing.

He'd spoken maybe two sentences since he'd brought her food up. And he didn't seem prepared to engage her in intelligent conversation now.

She squeezed her eyes shut as he pulled her shirt down and pressed his chest against her back, his cheek resting on her cheek. Her breathing came ragged as he held her this way, no words passing between them.

After an excruciating length of time, he released her. Her arms were sore from being held up so long.

His mouth brushed her ear. "Run."

Her body had refused the order when it came direct from her own brain, but from his lips, it sent her scurrying up the stairs. She didn't stop until she reached the tower, even though she felt her lungs might burst from the trip. Mina sat on the edge of her bed, staring at the door, waiting for it to open and hoping it wouldn't, listening to the rapid thumping of her heart.

Lost in the world of dreams, Mina forgot the deal she'd made with the doctor, the long trip to the house, and Brian. She dreamed of normal things. Going to the bakery. Buying a new coffeemaker. Doing her taxes. The kind of dream so boring, its content—if it could be bottled—would cure the world's insomnia.

Upon waking and finding herself in the tower, she had a sense of inversion, as if reality had flipped. Weren't things like this supposed to be the dream while boring monotony was meant to be real life?

She'd read the book of rules cover to cover several times the previous night, trying to calm her heart rate, trying to focus on anything but Brian's intense dark stare, trying to forget the sound of his voice when he told her to run.

She was no stranger to various BDSM protocols, but Jason had made it all more sinister. Somehow in Dr. Smith's office, she'd indulged in the fantasy that with the right man Jason could be erased. In therapy she'd tried to get to the root of where her submissive feelings sprang.

They were obviously incompatible with reality. No matter what she said she wanted, no matter what she longed for and tried to articulate, gentleness was never on the menu for long when they realized they couldn't *fix* her and make her want sex in the *normal way*, or the *normal way* with kink layered on top. Jason had punished her the worst for the infraction of simply not liking something. He might have totally lost his mind had she told him she wasn't fond of chocolate. Because, like intercourse, everybody liked chocolate. If they weren't weirdos.

Now, instead of running from that lifestyle like the pestilence it was, she'd run headlong into this extreme version of it. The version where it was real—because it wouldn't be a game. She'd really belong to someone. Actual money would change hands. The promise from someone she'd foolishly grown to trust of the one thing she hadn't been able to find on her own had made her brain shut down its rational faculties.

Mina startled when the door opened and dropped to the floor on her knees, her head down. The rulebook had been clear that when morning came on her first day they were operating at full protocol, and disobedience would be punished. After seeing the dungeon downstairs and her close brush with Brian, she'd mentally sworn she wouldn't break any rules. Whatever it took, she couldn't be sent to him.

Deep down she knew nothing would keep her safe. It hadn't with Jason or those before him. Jason had made up fake rules that she'd supposedly broken to justify punishment. Or else he claimed he had needs, and she was the slave, and she was supposed to please him. So if he wanted to spend a couple of hours beating the shit out of her and passing her around to his grubby friends, well, she should just be thrilled for the honor. Because didn't subs like that shit? And what was wrong with her if she didn't like it, too?

He'd gone so far once as to accuse her of being a vanilla tease, claiming she had grand fantasies but in the end withheld things. But she hadn't. She'd given him everything he wanted, and it still hadn't been enough because what he'd wanted was to rewire her brain as if it were his own personally-written software. She was a broken line of code he couldn't fix. In the end he was disappointed that she was a real person instead of a fantasy in his head that followed his script to the letter.

She pushed down her revulsion as black shiny boots entered her field of vision. *Please don't be Brian. Please don't be Brian.*

"Good girl. What's next?"

"Lindsay." Thank God. She crawled to him and kissed his boots. It wasn't Brian. That was enough. There was a time when every rule in the binder would have made her wet. Now she wondered if she could get excited at all. A flash of her time with Anton at *Dome* flitted through her mind, and she felt herself flush.

"Sir," he barked. "In this house, everyone is Sir, do you understand?"

"Y-yes Sir." It wasn't as if she hadn't read that line sixteen times. She'd just forgotten. This was a bad idea. She couldn't be here. "Please, I-I want to go home. I-I was wrong. This isn't for me."

Warm hands wrapped around hers and pulled her to stand. He lifted her face to his. "You can never be set free. You've seen too much, and you know it. You agreed. You can't go back on it now."

"Please . . . I can't . . ."

"Don't speak another word until I give you permission."

Mina closed her mouth and dropped her gaze. Even if prolonged eye contact weren't prohibited in the book of rules, it would be far too intimate. She needed the space and privacy to figure out how she'd endure what would likely be a fate orders of magnitude worse than Jason.

Lindsay took her to a large suite on the second floor. When the door shut, she glanced furtively around. Lindsay's room. It had to be. It was a jungle of plants—many of them green and leafy. Others were exotics, including orchids like in his office. The plants grew under artificial lights with *rain* coming out of tubes in the ceiling to water them. The water swirled down drains in the floor. The main part of the floor, away from the plants was dark green carpet that made her feel like she was in a jungle. There was a king-sized canopy bed with a dark green duvet and mosquito netting around the outside.

As if that weren't enough, there were several large bird cages with parakeets as well as one with an African Grey parrot.

"Yes, Sir. Oh harder harder. Just like that . . . I'm going to cooooooooome," the parrot said.

Mina laughed. She hadn't laughed in a long time. The sound felt foreign.

"Enough, Ralph," the doctor said, covering the cage.

"Enough. Enough. Enough. Yes, Sir. Enough."

"Ignore him," Lindsay said. "He likes the attention."

The doctor led Mina to the bed and spun her to face him. He lifted her face again and held her gaze. The smile lines around his eyes weirdly calmed her. He bent and captured her mouth in a kiss, and for perhaps the thousandth time she wanted to belong to him—not some stranger she couldn't trust.

"Please, can't I be yours? I don't care if you don't have time for me. We're here now. I'll take whatever you can give."

Lindsay's eyes narrowed. "I took a big chance on you. If you want to live without pain, you have to be able to follow basic instructions. I told you not to speak until I gave you permission. Did I give you permission?"

"No, Sir."

"You set boundaries that make it impossible to punish you, then you can't give me the courtesy of basic obedience? It was a simple request. Keep your mouth shut until I tell you to speak. Is that clear?"

From laughter to tears in thirty seconds. "Y-yes, Sir. I-I'm sorry."

The previous night she'd had no problem not speaking. Brian's mere presence seemed to shut down her ability to do much of anything.

"Undress."

She couldn't imagine with Lindsay's anger that what was coming would be the sweet gentleness she'd hoped for. He would fuck her. Or beat her. Or some combination of the two. She never should have trusted him.

But here she was, locked away in a monstrous house where no one would help her. She unbuttoned and removed the top, her eyes trained on the floor. The pajama pants and her panties joined the pile.

He took her hand more gently than she expected—considering his anger—and took her to the large walk-in closet. Inside was a cage. He pressed a code into a metal box attached to the side, and the door opened. The cage was shorter than she was but wide enough to sit and move. Thick, black metal bars made up the walls and top. The bottom was solid.

"Inside," Lindsay said.

Mina didn't argue. She was too afraid of how much things could escalate if she tried to refuse her punishment. She was sure if she hadn't disobeyed him that things would have gone much differently in his plant room. On the floor was a red button.

The metal door locked behind her.

"Push that button at your own risk," he said. "It's for emergencies only. You press it; someone will come. If they don't like your reason for pushing it, you'd better pray to every god you've ever heard of."

She wanted to scream that he was just like the others, but she was afraid to say anything. She was hungry, and she needed a cigarette. How long would he keep her in here?

He turned off the lights, closed the door, and his footsteps receded back to the main house.

Brian regretted demanding a day off. After seeing Mina last night downstairs, he wanted nothing more than to stay and hurt someone. His sleep had been more troubled than usual, the memories wrapping around inside his mind like twisting vipers, creating dreams he felt sure were more vivid than it had been in reality.

He needed to get out of the house, get some fresh air. Go into the city. Forget this place for a while. He slowed as he passed Lindsay's office.

"Where is she?" Gabe asked.

"In the cage in my closet. Hold onto this. Go to her if she pushes the button."

Brian didn't have to see inside the office to know it was a black receiver box.

"When will you be back?"

"I have a few appointments. If I'm not back, let her out around noon."

Brian continued down the hallway and detoured through the cafeteria. He took a secondary staircase to the second floor. Lindsay's door was unlocked, no doubt so Gabe could reach Mina if necessary, but it also gave Brian access. His day off could wait.

As he approached the closet, he heard her crying. He slipped inside the darkness, shutting the door before she could look up. She went deadly quiet, like she had down-stairs with him the night before. Did she know it was him?

She saw what he was in a way few others had. Sure, they were all afraid of him, but usually only after they'd been given a reason to fear: being sent down for a punishment, observing the reactions of other girls, rumors at the lunch table. By contrast, Mina had reacted like a frightened doe the moment she'd seen him—even when he wasn't being particularly threatening. Her instincts unnerved him.

He'd thought he wanted her to be afraid, but the marks on her back were like a mystical shield of protection. It put her on his team. It made her his co-captive in need of justice and protection. Brian didn't know what to do with these thoughts and feelings. He'd never had them before. He didn't welcome them, but he couldn't push them away. He couldn't push *her* away.

When he managed to stop the circle his thoughts ran around, the darkness of the closet engulfed him, and for a moment the room went hot, and he couldn't breathe. He was trapped under the stairs again. He gripped a shelf that held Lindsay's casual khaki pants. Mina gasped at the sound, clearly working to hold in her own panic.

He tried to steady his breath, tried not to hyperventilate, tried not to be that weak, scared child again crying out in the dark for someone to help and protect him.

He'd wanted to come in under cover of darkness. He'd wanted to touch the side of her face and have her lean toward him through the bars, not knowing it was him. He'd never wanted a woman to come to him willingly, to trust him. He'd never cared and thought any woman who trusted him was foolish and deserved whatever she got. But Mina was different. He wanted to know what one moment of tenderness given or received could feel like even as he berated himself for the thought.

But the darkness swallowed him. He wanted to flee, but he couldn't bring himself to leave her behind.

He took a slow, shuddering breath and flipped the light on. Just a normal walk-in closet. Everything was fine. He was large and strong. Six foot four. Broad. Even grown men walked the other way when he moved down the street. Nothing could hurt him anymore. He composed himself and turned toward her.

Mina scooted as far as she could into one of the back corners of the cage, which admittedly wasn't very far.

He approached and sat cross-legged next to her. When she started to edge away, his voice stopped her.

"There's nowhere for you to go. I'll be annoyed if I have to chase you around the cage."

She stopped her retreat, still trembling. "P-please, Sir . . . I didn't push the button. I didn't push it."

"I know you didn't."

She wouldn't stop shaking.

It bothered him more than he liked to see her huddled in the cage. Some sinister part of him rebelled, wanting to hurt her for whatever it was about her that made him feel compassion for a woman he didn't even know. But the greater part of him—for possibly the first time ever—rebelled against that notion so strongly that the thought of it almost made him physically ill.

Instead, he found himself saying, "Do you need anything?"

Her face was guarded, as if she were looking for the trap. He didn't blame her. If it had been any other girl, the trap would have been set and waiting. But there was no trap this time.

Brian raised his voice. "When I ask you a question, I expect an answer. Do you know who I am?"

"N-no, Sir."

"No you don't need anything or no you don't know who I am?"

"The latter."

Interesting. She still had no idea of his role in the house. Why would Lindsay bring someone here that was so damaged? Did he really think he could find someone suitable to buy her? This girl was too far gone—not fit for anyone. And she couldn't be released back out into the wild. If Lindsay had wanted her for himself, he should have taken her, rather than engage in this charade.

"Do you need anything?"

"B-bathroom," she whispered.

He input the code on the cage. When the door opened, he reached inside to take her hand.

She remained pressed against the corner. So still. The weird thing was, he was only now noticing she was naked. That should have been his first observation. Ordinarily he would have taken it all in and been gleeful about his find and all the depraved and sadistic things he could do—both sexual and non-sexual—to his captive. But with Mina, the overriding thought in his mind had been that she was in a cage, and he didn't want her there. In fact, it began to irritate and grate on him, causing that burning itch that usually only hurting someone stopped.

"It would be better for you if you come out on your own."

Mina considered this, then slowly crawled out. She hesitated before her lips brushed over his boot. She didn't attempt to rise until he helped her up and led her to Lindsay's bathroom.

"I'll wait out here." Another thing he wouldn't normally give a woman here . . . privacy. What was going on with him?

The lock clicked over, and he wondered if she might stay in there all day, considering it a safer cage to be in where he was concerned. But when she finished, she came back out. Her hair fell over her face as she looked down, and the trembling starting again. He didn't say a word as he led her back to the closet and into the cage.

She didn't go to the corner this time. Instead she chose the center of the enclosure. He could reach her if he stretched, but not as easily as when she'd been pressed against the bars. He watched while she stared at the bottom of the cage.

If he let her go, Lindsay would be furious and probably punish her worse. If he took her down to the dungeon suite, he'd have a fight on his hands with the other partners—since it had been decided without his input once again that a girl here was off limits to him.

Brian retrieved his cell from his pocket and dialed Lindsay from the contact list. The doctor answered on the first ring.

"I'm currently standing in the walk-in closet with your newest caged acquisition. She's naked. She's vulnerable. And she can't get away from me. Three of my favorite things. You might consider rescuing her before I decide to get creatively sadistic. Just a thought."

Brian hung up and waited. It didn't take long.

Less than five minutes later, the door flung open to reveal Gabe full of puffed-up righteous indignation, as if he'd somehow been personally slighted by this.

"Lindsay said you knew you weren't allowed near her," Gabe said, the rage barely concealed. Let him be angry. This house didn't function properly without Brian. Good luck getting these lightweights to enact any real discipline.

Brian raised an eyebrow. "I'm sorry, since when do I obey your orders? I'm an equal partner here, or have you all forgotten? I may live underground, but that doesn't make me some low-ranking servant. You don't get to keep any girl within these walls from me. Just because I more or less stayed away from Vivian doesn't mean that's the precedent we're going to follow. If Lindsay didn't want me near her, he shouldn't have brought her here. Or he should have cleared his policy with me, first."

"You can't touch Anton's slave," the blond said.

"Annette has a collar. She belongs exclusively to him. I respect that claim. Mina, however, has no such collar to protect her. Tell Lindsay to leave her locked up alone anywhere in this house at his own risk." He moved forward, invading Gabe's space. "Have you read the contract for her?"

Gabe gritted his teeth. "I have."

"Then know this. I will break every boundary in that contract if I find her in such a vulnerable position again. Every. Boundary." He turned to Mina, who shrank back. "What was the crime that got you put in the cage?"

"I-I spoke without permission, S-sir."

Brian turned back to the blond. "A rebel, this one. Certainly it was worth the risk I pose to her."

"Isn't it your day off?"

"It depends. If you're leaving her in the cage, I'm playing with her. What about the remotes for her bracelet?"

Most of the trainers kept a small remote that allowed them to send a shock to a bracelet. It was an effective form of training and punishment.

"Her bracelet hasn't been programmed that way. The remotes won't work."

Was that relief Brian felt?

Gabe shoved past him and input the code. "It's all right, Mina," he said as he helped her out.

He took a blanket from one of the shelves and wrapped her up to help stop her shaking. Brian had wanted to do the very same thing, but it would have looked strange, and he didn't want the third degree. It was easier to play to type. He got what he wanted, and nobody thought he'd gone insane. It was better that he try to come to terms with his odd reaction to her on his own.

Brian caught Mina's gaze. "Don't wander alone in this house. I might not be able to keep my hands off you. Ask Gabe; he'll tell you what I do with these hands. You and your delicate sensibilities wouldn't like it."

He watched as she moved closer to Gabe for his protection—such that it was. Then he turned and left Lindsay's room and the house, trying hard to get the dark, fragile beauty out of his mind.

Four

Mina watched Brian's retreating form. Empirically he'd freed her—an obvious kindness. Yet he'd threatened her as well. But he could have acted on it before calling Lindsay. Why hadn't he? She shook her head to clear it. She knew this. It was the same set of games Jason had played. Gain the captive's trust with small kindnesses mixed with a touch of cruelty to keep her off guard. Find the most entertaining moment . . . and strike, unraveling any sense of safety she ever had.

If she'd learned these lessons with the first three men —abusive amateurs next to Jason—she might have salvaged some of her dignity and unscarred skin. But she'd learned the lesson well enough with Jason that Brian wouldn't succeed in the same con. Though if she'd truly learned it, she wouldn't have trusted Lindsay and come here in the first place. Surely now she was cured of any remaining remnants of her so-called *kink*.

Brian was devastatingly handsome, but more importantly, he was devastating.

His home in the dungeon, his warning to run, his threats this morning, all gave voice to support the instinctive fear she'd felt the moment she'd first entered his presence. She didn't plan to give him another opportunity alone with her. And she wouldn't give Lindsay or any of the others the opportunity to lock her up and risk another run-in with Brian.

Gabe went into the main bedroom and came back with her clothes. "Get dressed and come down for breakfast while they're still serving it. Lindsay canceled his appointments for the day. He's on his way back."

Mina dressed faster than she'd ever dressed and rushed to get down the stairs to a place that was more crowded, for fear that Brian might still be lurking. But he was nowhere to be found.

The scene that greeted her in the cafeteria was surreal. There were several girls, all around college age, in cliques at a couple of tables having breakfast. They looked normal enough. Kind of a *mean girls* vibe. Other tables were less normal. Some of the girls were naked, with men hanging all over them. Some were being touched by multiple men, fingers penetrating them while they tried to have breakfast.

She looked away.

It wasn't that she'd never seen public sexual things. It was just that this was broad daylight, with the sunlight streaming in and a view of a pool out back. And while the kink clubs might have had nudity and bondage and whipping, there was something subtly different here. There was no sex in public at the clubs, but it seemed certain it was about to start happening here. At least at that one table.

Mina tried to quiet the urges that woke within her. Her body demanded this. But the price was too high to pay. She'd been kidding herself if she thought any kind of happy relationship lay ahead of her. Even before therapy and Lindsay's offer, the hope of anything but loneliness and fear around men had been a fantasy—a fevered daydream she'd foolishly tried to make real. Again.

Mina got eggs, bacon, juice, and a bran muffin and sat as far from everyone else as she could get. She imagined herself a chameleon, fading into the chair so she wouldn't call the attention either of the mean girls at the center table, or the men engaged in the breakfast orgy.

The blond who'd rescued her from Brian, approached as she was finishing and putting her tray away. "Lindsay's back. He wants to speak with you in his office."

Something inside her sank. After their earlier interaction, any hope she'd had that the doctor would keep her himself was gone. Now she wasn't sure she even wanted him. This wasn't a game, and even the smallest lapse in formality might earn her another punishment just as upsetting as being beaten. If so many things upset her, what did any of her preferences or urges in men even mean?

The doctor seemed impatient when she reached his office, as if she hadn't flown there fast enough for his taste.

"Please shut the door and sit." He indicated a chair.

The relationship they'd had as doctor and patient had evaporated, leaving in its wake something she wasn't sure she liked at all. The freedom she'd felt to speak her mind—to address him even—was gone now.

Lindsay was silent for a long while as he seemed to gather his words together in a bundle. "Mina, I believe bringing you here was an error on my part. Even with all the therapy sessions, I'm not sure I truly realized the extent of the damage that's been done to you. I wanted to help you. And in truth, I wanted to help myself. It was a conflict of interests even for me."

She opened her mouth but then remembered herself and stopped short.

"You may speak freely inside this office. It's still a therapist's office, and without that freedom you can't be helped."

"You said you couldn't let me go back home. What does this mean for me?" Surely he wasn't going to have her killed. That would hardly be more kind than the situation he'd already initiated.

"My plan was to put you through the standard training protocol, keeping in mind the boundaries we agreed to. However, I realized this morning that without pain as a tool, punishments become more challenging. And with Brian in the house . . . I can't risk you with him. I find that I have a personal fondness toward you that clouds my vision."

Again, the question of why *he* couldn't keep her bubbled to the surface.

"Before you say it again, I can't collar you. It exposes you constantly to the danger of Brian. He respects Anton's claim on Annette, but . . . he's taken an unusual interest in you. I can't speak about his past. It would betray doctor/patient confidentiality, but I can tell you that you are not safe near him."

She couldn't argue with that logic. Though Brian had yet to hurt her, he felt like a bomb that had already been set to go off. It was merely a matter of the clock winding down to zero.

"W-where does that leave us? If you let me go back home, I swear I won't say anything about anything."

Lindsay shook his head. "I'm afraid that's not an option. I intend to go ahead and find a buyer for you and get you out of the house within the next day or two. I went through my business contacts late last night, and there are several potential candidates who have bought other girls from us and who I trust implicitly with your safety. A few of them prefer their own training protocols, so your untrained state won't be an issue."

Mina was offended by his *untrained state* comment. It too closely echoed Jason's *not a real sub* accusation. How could she be untrained if she'd lived in so many 24/7 D/s arrangements in the past? Though had she? If such arrangements existed and ever worked out, she hadn't been lucky enough to be one of the participants. From her view and experience, it had been a nice shady corner for abusive men to hide in. And now she'd moved to the next level of the same fucking thing.

Why couldn't she let her fantasies stay fantasies instead of insisting on finding a way to act them out and live them?

The doctor continued. "I'll ask that you stay in the tower until it's time for you to leave us. You may lock your door. I have a feeling it's the only thing that will keep Brian out. Your meals will be brought up. Again, I want to apologize for everything, and I promise I will do my very best to find a good match for you, somewhere you can be happy. I can at least assure that you will be safe. Do you have any questions?"

"C-can I get some cigarettes?" Earlier in the cage, at least part of the shaking had been the need of a cigarette. With the stress and uncertainty of her future, she didn't want to think about how bad the withdrawal might get.

"No. There will be no smoking here. You won't be allowed to smoke once you're sold, so it's better to work through the cravings and discomfort now. You may go."

Lindsay returned to the stack of papers in front of him, effectively dismissing her from his life forever.

When Mina reached the door, his voice stopped her. "To ensure your care and safety, and because you've been my patient, I'll see you once a week if you still want that. I'll arrange it with the buyer. We can do video conferencing."

"Okay."

She felt numb, empty, afraid, the fantasy once again unraveling—this time before it started.

"Oh, and one more thing."

"Yes?"

"I'll need to do a health examination and take some photos and video for the auction. You won't be required to be present for the sale. Everything will be handled behind the scenes."

"Photos and video?" Mina wasn't sure she was comfortable with that, but she hadn't thought to set *no photos or video of me* as a limit. That kind of thing could end up anywhere. It could come back to haunt her.

"They have to see what they're buying. Would you rather be displayed naked on the conference table and be poked and prodded by myself or Gabe or Anton while bidders look on? Would you rather risk Brian being present for the event and touching you, too?"

She shuddered. No. She didn't want to risk any of that. When Lindsay first suggested finding a master for her, and he'd mentioned money changing hands, what had she thought he meant? If it was enough money to bother, of course potential buyers would want to see what they were paying for. Of course she'd be treated like an object on the auction block. Wasn't not having to be physically present a mercy?

There was a time when the idea would have excited her, but now . . . If being here had taught her anything, it was that Jason had truly broken her. Could even a kind master, following the rules of the contract, have any hope of reawakening her? Could she trust anyone to open that side of herself up again?

For months in therapy she'd focused on what she couldn't have. She'd obsessed about it and held onto it. Now, presented with it, she began to wonder why she'd been so fixated. Maybe she was meant to be single with some cats. But it was too late for that. She'd signed her rights away. And Lindsay would enforce that choice to save his own ass. Only now, if she fought, he couldn't hide behind the cloak of doing something noble and kind for her—of fulfilling all her fantasies and giving her everything she'd ever wanted.

If she fought now, it would be ugly and brutal for both of them. He'd be her captor and kidnapper. She'd be his victim. She couldn't bring herself to be anyone else's victim again right now. If she went along, maybe she could find that place inside herself that actually liked this idea.

"Come on, it'll be all right, Mina. I'm sorry to have to do this to you. If you knew how rarely I apologized to anyone for anything, you'd know my sincerity. It was foolish to bring you here, and now I've started a chain of events I can't release myself or you from. If it comforts you, everyone at the auction will be a previous buyer— someone the house has a history with and who has honored our contracts in the past. You need not fear anyone who might buy you."

Lindsay led her to the end of the hallway.

"W-wait . . . we're doing this right now?"

In answer, he unlocked the door and pushed her inside. The room looked like it moonlighted as a porn set. A medical examining area, including a table and stirrups, was set up in the back corner. There was lighting and camera equipment everywhere. The center of the room was a simple bed with fluffy white bedding and steel bars for a headboard.

Lindsay pressed a button on the wall intercom.

"Yes?" Anton's thick accent caressed the air.

"I need you in the auction prep room."

"Give me fifteen."

Lindsay turned on the lights—not just the normal lights in the ceiling or the ambient lamps strategically placed around the room, but also the studio lighting.

"Get on the examining table. I need to take samples for analysis."

Mina wore the white t-shirt and colorful gym shorts the girls of the house had been given for casual free time. It was weird to think that she'd yet to be involved in anything overtly sexual herself here. She felt like a nun, stumbling upon somebody's porn stash. The only thing resembling BDSM had been the naked cage incident.

She sat on the exam table as the doctor took off his sport coat and replaced it with a white lab coat. He scrubbed up in the sink and pulled on blue medical gloves. He set up a tray with a syringe and alcohol and cotton swabs.

"I'm going to swipe under your tongue for a mineral and hormone profile. Then I'll draw blood to do a full blood panel. After that I'll do the gynecological exam. We'll do photos and video both here and on the bed. Anton will join us for part of it."

She'd become so consumed with her fears and the knowledge she had of how deeply her trust could be abused, that she'd forgotten the erotic charge of *a little* fear. Previous men had never dwelled in that space of erotic fear. They'd pushed right past that. Anticipation had changed to terror, and the mild flutter of flushed excitement had never returned. But inside this room with the doctor, she thought maybe it could melt back into anticipation.

"A-are you going to videotape t-the exam?"

"Not the boring parts, but yes. There will be no hospital gown as you may be used to in these types of things. Don't you think your master has the right to see everything in the exam?"

"Y-yes Sir."

Lindsay touched her cheek. "We will find you someone. He will meet your needs for a master who won't harm you. Everything you've been through up to this point will have been worth it. Just trust me."

Lindsay sealed the saliva sample in a bag, then took the needle from the tray and drew blood. When he finished, he put a label on the vial and put it in a bag as well. He jotted notes on a chart inside a manilla folder. Then he put everything he'd gathered into a larger plastic bag.

She startled when the door opened, but it was only Anton. He moved behind the video equipment like a shadow. He adjusted it to view the examining table. Then he set up the photography equipment.

"Mina," Lindsay said. "I want you to undress, lie back on the table, and put your feet in the stirrups for me."

She'd thought she could do this. She'd wanted to believe. She'd tried so hard to believe that everything inside her hadn't been broken already, that the pieces could somehow be glued back together so that no one would ever even notice.

She wanted the fantasy to work. She wanted to trust one more time. She'd thought she'd felt those hints that her body still wanted this, and maybe it did. But her mind couldn't take any more of it. If only she'd known this the day the driver came. She wouldn't have chased him. She would have let him go. But seeing those tail lights had made her panic . . . like this was her last chance for . . . anything. She knew it.

And she was so lonely. How could she go on this way? If some kind man could take her and remake her and heal her . . . She just wanted to believe the fantasy. That was all. Just one more time.

"N-no, I-I can't."

The doctor's eyes narrowed. Something in his expression snapped apart and the mask came off. His voice went dark and low as if a demon had taken possession of him. "What did you just say to me? Maybe I should send you down to Brian. A couple of hours in the dungeon with him, and you'll be grateful to do anything I ask of you in here. A couple of hours with him and you'd let every man in this house do anything he wanted with you and feel honored for the privilege. Believe me, you would do anything to stay out of one of his cells. You think you're scared of me? Anton? This? You think this is too much for you? I've fucking had it with you!"

Mina dropped to her knees. "Please . . . I'm sorry I c-can't. Please don't make me do those things. Please. I swear I won't tell anyone if you just let me go."

Lindsay laughed. "Let you go? No my dear, you are in deep now. There is no going except to a master or a pine box. Your choice. I could make you do this. I can just strip you and tie you down, but the buyers we might attract with such footage wouldn't be the ones you'd want."

"Lindsay. Stop! Stop this! Just go cool off," Anton said, pulling the doctor back.

Lindsay wrenched out of his grasp and stormed from the room, slamming the door behind him. Mina flinched when Anton helped her up.

"I should have told him no when he asked about you. When you came to *Dome*, I was going to do more, but I couldn't. You had so much fear coming off you. Even with the excitement, it was too much fear. I thought he would kill you, so I said yes. He knows he's made a big mistake and that you don't deserve to die for it. Let me talk to him. I'll try to calm him down."

When Anton left, Mina curled up in the bed in the middle of the room. She hoped the sheets were clean, but she didn't care. She just wanted to disappear. She cringed and clenched the blankets over her head as the shouting in the hallway grew louder. The walls were thick, so she couldn't make out what they were saying, but she could imagine.

After a while the shouting became loud talking, and then a murmur of normal speech. And then silence. The door opened again. Lindsay walked back in, composed, Anton behind him. Anton stood in the corner while Lindsay pulled a chair up to sit beside the bed.

"Here is how it will be," the doctor said. "I have to have photos of something. No one will buy you sight unseen. So we are going to do photos that aren't nude. Just normal everyday pictures. I will speak to my contacts and explain the new development in this situation to see if I can find anyone who will be patient with you long term, who can accept that you might be far too broken to ever be anything more than their maid. Can you clean? Can you cook?"

Mina couldn't meet his eyes. "Y-yes, Sir."

"Good. Because it's probably about all you're good for."

"W-why can't I just stay here?"

"We are not going to feed and house you as a permanent guest. You have no use in this house. And you think Brian is going to resist the temptation to fuck you up beyond repair? You think Jason was bad? Jason is an amateur next to Brian. Brian is a full-on sociopath. If he wasn't doing this, he'd probably be a serial killer. Can you tell me you want to stay in a house with a man like that and risk your paths crossing?"

"N-no, Sir."

"I didn't think so. I'll do what I can. Just pray I can make a deal. If I can't . . ."

If he couldn't he'd have her killed.

Brian got back to the house well after dark. He hadn't been able to stop thinking about Mina. In an unsettling turn of events, he'd come to see himself as her protector. The idea of protecting Mina from *Lindsay* was so absurd, he almost laughed out loud in the entryway.

He was about to go downstairs when he heard voices coming from the conference room next to the shrink's office. That was . . . odd. There wasn't a meeting scheduled. Were they having meetings without him now? Things had been tense with the partners ever since Vivian. It was as if her presence—and his threat—had finally set them against each other in a more permanent way.

They were all on one team; Brian was alone on the other. Which was ridiculous. They couldn't do this shit without him. And they knew it.

"What in the hell is going on?" he demanded when he crossed the threshold.

The partners were seated around the table with Lindsay at the head, clearly running this meeting, which was weird because usually Anton ran the meetings. Attached to empty seats around the table were computer monitors where several men had joined the video conference. Brian recognized them all as previous buyers.

Several modest photographs of Mina fully clothed were scattered across the large table. If Lindsay was running it like a normal sale, the potential buyers had been emailed their own copies as well. But it wasn't a normal sale because the photos they normally shared were pornographic. Even their medical photos were sexualized and would be at home under the bed of any fetishist who got off on the darker implications of gynecology.

Not innocent like this.

What the hell was going on?

"Gentlemen, I apologize for the interruption," Lindsay said. He turned to Brian. "We're holding the auction now."

"For Mina?" he asked unnecessarily. It was too soon for this. It didn't feel right, and those photos . . . Something was very wrong. In the pictures, it looked like she'd been crying.

"Yes."

Brian's stomach dropped, but he masked it with anger. "She hasn't even gone through the training protocols. Are you that worried about what I'll do to her?"

"Our guests are aware of her state of training and the nature of the contract. We're all agreed that many of our training protocols would be useless in this unique circumstance and that it's better to go ahead and sell her to a trusted buyer who can work with her from the ground up and protect her in ways we might not be able to. And yes, her safety from you is of paramount import-ance to me. I'm sure you won't guarantee her safety, will you?"

It was looking more and more as if Mina were the singular person in all the world who Brian might be able to successfully guarantee safety to. The idea of her being ripped away so soon—before he could sort through his feelings—enraged him. He pulled out a chair and sat at the table uninvited.

"Shall we start the bidding, then?" Lindsay said, ignoring him. "Given the special circumstances involved and that you are all valued clients, we'll start at the reas-onable bargain of one hundred thousand dollars."

"One hundred thousand," said a Japanese man on one of the screens.

Lindsay seemed quite pleased. "Thank you Mr. Matsumoto. Mina would do well to end up with you."

He nodded.

"Two-fifty," another said.

"Five hundred," Matsumoto said.

"Seven hundred," still another said.

Brian looked down to find himself white knuckling the edge of the table, his jaw clenched.

"One million," Matsumoto said.

Why did this guy want her so much? She was untrained. She had too many boundaries for the contract. And she had the scars. A hundred thousand was reason-able given the circumstances, and Matsumoto had just gone up to a million? Sure, Mina was beautiful, but something was wrong about this sale. Lindsay had rushed it. Was he sure about these guys?

Maybe Brian was paranoid. Why did he even care? The bidding somehow climbed to one and a half million with Matsumoto still in control.

"Two," Brian said, his mouth disconnecting from his brain entirely.

"What do you think you're doing?" Lindsay hissed.

Brian covered his own shock at the words that had just tumbled forth. He could still take it back, but instead he said, "Bidding. I've got the money." At the house all his needs were taken care of, and he got an equal cut with the other partners of all sales after house expenses and paying those in their employ. His money had been sitting around collecting interest.

"Is this some kind of shakedown?"

"No, I assure you, Mr. Matsumoto, that is not the case here. Brian, stay out of the bidding. I wouldn't sell Mina to you if you were the last man alive. Scrap Brian's bid, and we're back down to one and a half million to Mr. Matsumoto. Are there any other bids?"

The others shook their heads and bowed out. Matsumoto smiled broadly. The man who'd just won Mina might have followed the house rules up to this point, but Brian knew a predator and a sadist when he saw one. He could smell his own. There was something about the Mina situation that was bringing out a darker side to the man, one that Brian refused to allow to materialize.

"Five million," Brian said, "And you can keep my cut of it, personally, Lindsay."

Lindsay just blinked. Matsumoto looked livid. If the man had been there in person, a physical fight would have broken out. As it was, Matsumoto could only sit fuming behind the monitor. After all, it wouldn't do him any favors to unleash his rage for all of them to witness. It might bring into question his ability to hold his temper and control himself—things absolutely vital to Mina's safety.

If Brian knew Lindsay like he thought he did, this kind of offer was way too much money for him to leave on the table in favor of one less than a third as good.

"Gentlemen, I'm going to have to have a private meeting with my associates. Mr. Matsumoto, I will call back as soon as this is sorted. Again, I apologize for this unprofessional display."

"I told you I'm not selling her to you," Lindsay said after the conference call disconnected. "I don't know what sick games you want to play with her, but I made a promise."

"I won't hurt her. I'll follow the contract."

"If you believe him, you're crazy," Gabe said. "He was making threats toward her just this morning."

Anton observed quietly. He ran the meetings and arranged the sales, but Mina was Lindsay's pet project, and the doctor was determined to manage everything himself.

"I didn't want her locked in the cage," Brian said.

Lindsay raised a brow. "Why not?"

"I don't know! But I want her. Matsumoto will hurt her. Something's not right about his bid."

"Something's not right about your bid! In fact, your bid is far more shady than his. He's had Elsa in his care for six years without a single blip on our radar, and she seems fine. Meanwhile, I've never seen a woman leave your dungeon without an ugly mark to show for it!" Lindsay was shouting now, all attempts at restraint abandoned. "You expect me to believe you'd pay five million for this girl you just met who as you pointed out is untrained and that she'd be perfectly safe with you when you've shown me nothing but signs of sociopathy the entire time I've known you?"

"Where is she safest? Think about it. Off with Matsumoto half a world away, or right here under your own nose where you can keep an eye on her and me? What if I'm right about him?"

"Then we can find another buyer."

"It'll be too late. If you're wrong, she won't recover from it. She might not even survive it. You're not God, Lindsay. You can't peer into the hearts and minds of men and know who is safe and who isn't, no matter how much you've convinced yourself you have that power."

"Why would you pay this kind of money?"

"It means nothing to me. I have everything I need. I want her more than I want the money. What the fuck am I going to do with money when I never get a goddamned day off?"

Gabe and Anton just stared at him.

"Please," Brian said quietly.

"Did you just *beg* me to sell you Mina for five million dollars?"

"You might not trust my ability to keep my promises, but trust my ability to sense evil in someone else. I at least am good for that. Aren't I in this house because I bring things to the table that others don't? This is a part of what I bring."

"What do you guys think?"

Gabe and Anton shrugged.

"Why are you asking them?" Brian said. "They don't give a shit about her. You and I are the only ones invested."

"Just tell me why you want her."

Brian looked at the others then back to Lindsay. "Not in front of them."

"We'll go to my office."

Brian followed the doctor to his office and slumped into the chair across from his desk. Lindsay shut the door and joined him.

"Okay. Convince me."

In the privacy of the office everything felt too stark. Too honest. He looked up, unable to stop tears that were gathering. Fucking tears. He'd only cried in front of the shrink once during a particularly painful session. And he'd sworn he'd flat out murder the man if he ever breathed a word about seeing that weakness. Lindsay, to his credit, had believed the threat.

"I can't convince you. Just please let me have her. I won't hurt her. She's different." He couldn't bring himself to lay out why she was different, how from the moment he'd seen the scars on her back, she'd been under the stairs with him, how he was afraid violence alone wouldn't let him sleep anymore. The requirements for sleep had just escalated. Now he needed her, too. If Lindsay sent her to Japan, Brian might never sleep again.

"I'm going to need more than that," the doctor said.

"If I can protect her . . . I can erase it."

Lindsay's eyes narrowed. "Why would you care to erase what's been done to her?"

"No . . . me."

The light suddenly came on as the doctor grasped what he was saying. "She's a proxy for you. Interesting."

Brian wanted to kill him. Lindsay never stopped head shrinking and putting together his pet theories of why people were the way they were. As if knowing why changed anything or could make it different.

"Never mind. Forget it. I'm not going to sit here and beg you for her. She is mine. Either you take my money and we stay here, or I just take her and run."

The doctor stared hard at him as if looking for the bluff. He wouldn't find one. And he knew when he'd been beaten. "When do you want her?"

"Give me a week. I want to have a collar made, and I want the normal ceremony the other buyers get."

"You want it because you don't want her to see who's buying her and make a scene."

"Yeah," he said softly. "I don't want that."

Five

Mina huddled in bed, watching as the clock moved ominously toward eleven—the time she'd be sold off to a man she didn't know. She would have attempted escape if she'd thought such an action were possible, but the security was too tight.

After the scene with Lindsay in the medical room, she'd tried to avoid him and everyone else. He'd apologized for his behavior when he came to tell her she'd been sold. Sold. This nightmare would never end.

On top of everything else, she'd struggled for four days with tobacco withdrawal. It had been bad. It was hard to know if her current state of despair was because of her situation or the withdrawal. Probably both. No wonder people couldn't ever seem to quit. Now she just *wanted one*. Kind of like she wanted oxygen and sleep, but intellectually she knew she'd gotten through the worst of the withdrawal already.

Lindsay had given her a CD collection of Chopin during the worst of it. The music had calmed her somewhat. Was he still apologizing?

If he was doing that . . . why wasn't he keeping her? Obviously he cared in a way that went beyond doctor/patient.

But she'd seen his temper now. Did she want to stay with him anymore? No. The gift was part of the abuse cycle she'd suffered through too many times already. And the next man would be just the same.

Though she stayed mainly in her room, Lindsay insisted she at least needed exercise while she waited for the big day. He'd told her to swim in the pool after the others went to bed, assuring her that Brian never ventured upstairs that late. But how would he know? She still couldn't believe the doctor had threatened to send her to the dungeon.

Brian had been part of her motivation for staying in the tower and keeping the door locked. She couldn't let herself have another moment alone with him. She was too afraid of what he might do to her, given the chance.

But what of her master? What if he scared her just as badly as Brian did? As much as Lindsay had? There would be nowhere else to go from there.

A knock startled her out of her thoughts.

"Who is it?" She always asked before unlocking the door, still convinced Brian might be on the other side. But then, he seemed to have lost interest in her. He'd likely just been fucking with her head to scare her because it was easy. People like that saw a weakness and preyed on it. There was no begging them because they liked it.

"It's Annette, Anton's slave. I don't think we've formally met."

Mina opened the door and in swept a woman who looked shockingly like the receptionist at *Dome*—except that she wore a black leather collar with a silver ring attached to it.

"Do you work with Anton in the city?"

"Oh, no. That's my twin."

Annette held a black velvet box. She was flushed and excited.

"What's that?"

"It's your collar! Your master had it custom-designed. It's very nice—one of the nicest I've ever seen. You're going to love it."

Mina very much doubted she'd love her collar. There was nothing about this situation she loved. With every fiber of her being, she wished she had a time machine, that she could go back and refuse Lindsay's offer before it was too late and hope he didn't change his mind and decide she was a security threat.

Or better yet, she could take the time machine further and not visit the abusive doctor in the first place. And hell, if she were doing impossible magic time things, why not just go back to the very beginning and decide her fantasies were nice to masturbate to but there was no need to bring it into the real world and put herself at the mercy and hands of men who wouldn't protect her when it counted.

"Aren't you going to open it?"

Mina grimaced but opened the box. She didn't expect to be thrilled or impressed. The symbol of the stupidest decision of her life wasn't something she wanted to jump up and down about, but the piece of jewelry inside the box was the most perfect thing she'd ever seen.

It was a white metal: platinum, silver, white gold—she wasn't sure—with an intricate filigree design that went all the way around the band, and small, shimmering black stones. It was exactly like her grandmother's ring.

Mina looked from the collar to her ring and back again. "How?"

"Were you wearing the ring the day they did the pictures for the auction?"

"Yes." She'd never taken it off, and thankfully nobody asked her to.

"He must have noticed and requested one of the photos be enlarged."

She wanted to believe it was a sign. If the ring was a symbol of protection—even if it didn't work in the magical way it was supposed to—maybe the collar meant she'd be safe.

"You should put it on, now," Annette said.

When the collar clicked into place, a weird sort of peace settled over her. That feeling didn't last long.

Annette opened a drawer and pulled out a black and red corset, black panties, stockings, and a garter belt. "This is what you have to wear for the exchange." She opened another drawer and took out a pair of black heels. "I'm not sure if these will fit you. Try them."

They were a little tight. Annette helped her get ready, and then pulled out a blindfold. Mina shrank back.

"Anton said you might react this way, so I was sent up to smooth things. Normally it's my master or one of the other partners who does the exchange, but they thought you'd feel safer with me. They're big about ceremony around here. It's no big deal. But it'll be even easier for you. Normally you must verbally address your new master, which makes a lot of girls nervous, but the buyer has requested that part be left out. So all you have to do is make it across the floor to him. He expressed a desire to make this trade as easy on you as possible."

Anton's slave produced a silver ring the size of a bracelet. And a leash. She snapped the ring around the collar and attached the leash.

"I'll lead you into the hall where the exchange will be completed. When we reach the showroom, I'll nudge you, and you'll crawl across the floor to him. It's a carpeted floor so it won't be a big deal, and I'll lead you. You don't have to do anything formal. He's relaxed the rules for the exchange because he knows your history. All you have to do is kneel there silently while the documents are signed and everything is finalized. He'll feed you to complete the ceremony, then he'll lead you out."

Of course Anton's slave would make it sound like "not a big deal", but it was a very big deal. And he knew her history? What happened to the doctor/patient confidentiality Lindsay liked to crow about? It apparently didn't apply to slaves.

"W-what about the security bracelet?"

"Your master will take care of that once you're out of the showroom."

She hadn't even seen the man who'd bought her. What if he was hideous? What if he was cruel? What if he was crazy? And wasn't anyone who would do something like this automatically crazy? How much consent did he think she'd had in all this? She had no hope her boundaries would be honored. If the men she'd been in kink relationships with in the past hadn't managed to care about how she felt, then she knew someone who considered her his literal property with a receipt to prove it wouldn't care.

The only hope she had was that the house truly enforced the contracts and that she'd be able to let them know on their first visit how terrible everything was. If that was even true. Just because she'd seen Dr. Smith for months in his office didn't mean anything he'd told her about this house and the way it operated was true. In all likelihood, once she was out the door they wouldn't care what happened to her. Especially not after the trouble she'd caused.

"Please don't cry, you'll wreck your make-up," Annette said, wiping the tears that had started to fall. "It'll be okay."

But the lie was in her eyes. Annette was afraid. The girl knew something. Perhaps being Anton's slave gave her a look into the inner workings of the house that few others saw. She likely couldn't say anything without punishment, but her expression told Mina everything. She was about to step into the pit of Hell.

"Help me get out of here," Mina begged.

"I can't. The security band would electrocute you. It'll just escalate until you're unconscious and stop running. I've seen it happen."

It was becoming clear why the bracelet stayed on until the last possible second.

"J-just obey him. Don't make him angry."

"You've met him, haven't you?" Not only had Anton's slave probably met him, but she knew he had a temper. Had he made some sort of scene? Maybe not wanting Mina to speak wasn't for her comfort but because he didn't want her to speak. Ever.

Annette didn't reply. Instead she tied the blindfold in place and led her from the room.

"W-what about my things? Lindsay said to pack."

"We'll send your things as soon as you get settled," Annette said softly, trying to soothe her. But nothing would soothe her. And right now she didn't believe she'd ever see her things again. As if that mattered anymore.

"Come on. You just have to get through this. It will work out." But there was nothing convincing about her words. They were programmed, commanded words— simply a script she followed to avoid punishment from her own master.

Unlike the other times Mina had descended the endless stairs to get to the ground level, this trip felt like it took no time at all. In fact, time seemed to speed up to deliver her to her doom that much quicker.

Annette nudged her and she dropped to her hands and knees to crawl across the thick, plush carpet following the direction she was pulled.

When they stopped, Annette spoke. "S-sir, may I present your slave, Mina."

If this man made someone who lived here and saw everything stutter . . .

Mina couldn't stop the tears from sliding down her face. And all she could think was that she might already be making him angry by not appearing happy and eager to be there. Would she be punished for these tears once he got her out from under the watchful eye of the house? How far would they travel to get to wherever he planned to keep her?

She flinched when a large hand cupped her cheek, and a thumb wiped tears away. She could hear quiet conversation between the buyer and someone else. Mina assumed final papers were being signed. A moment later a grape was pressed into her mouth. And then a strawberry. She heard liquid being poured into a glass. He seemed to be leisurely sipping something. Wine perhaps? Maybe champagne to congratulate himself on his acquisition.

After several long minutes he stood and tugged the leash, taking her back in the direction she'd come in. She wanted to scream. She didn't care about the spectacle, but she was too afraid of what they'd do to her if she embarrassed them. Whoever this was had paid a lot of money. People with large sums of money to throw away on frivolity were often extremely entitled. She'd seen as much on a nightly basis as a waitress.

If she stepped out of line now, nothing would save her. She had to appease him and not make him angry. Maybe this person had a soul somewhere in there. Maybe she could reach it and find some softer part of him to appeal to.

It was the plan she'd employed with Jason and the other three before him. The plan hadn't worked then, and it wouldn't work now. She knew it. But it was all she had to hold onto.

When they reached the edge of the carpet and her knees hit harder floor, he helped her to stand, then he swept her up in his arms. She could do nothing but lay her head on his shoulder as he took her . . . to a waiting car?

She felt his strength as he carried her like she was nothing.

Mina didn't hear the outside door open. In fact, they were going too far, and now they were moving down. Down. The dungeons were down. Why weren't they leaving?

Panic seized her, but the man only gripped her tighter. When they reached solid ground, he moved with purpose several more steps, then opened a large, creaking door. He set her down on a bed as the door shut with a heavy thud.

She knew where she was, but she couldn't admit it. She refused to admit it. Lindsay didn't want her so she was supposed to be leaving the house, not be taken further inside it. It was quiet. Too quiet. Had she been left alone in here?

A weird part of her brain—probably for survival reasons—began to concoct a wild story about Lindsay having mercy on her, the sale being a ruse. He'd keep her somewhere hidden to secretly get her out later. She'd promise never to breathe a word of anything, and Lindsay would believe her and allow her to go back home.

If she just kept the blindfold on . . . if he didn't speak, she could keep the fantasy a little longer.

But he wouldn't allow such a kindness. Instead, he ripped the cloth away and she was face to face with the man she'd feared most in this house.

Brian watched her, his arms crossed over his chest.

"W-where's my master?" She didn't know where the bravery to speak had come from, and she'd known the answer before she spoke, but she was willing to grasp at anything—even the idea of some fictitious master out there who'd been somehow thwarted by Brian.

"I'm your master."

Even though she knew, even though she'd suspected from the moment they'd started descending the stairs . . . until he verbalized it, she'd taken refuge in denial and unlikely scenarios to explain it all away.

That was the fear in Annette's eyes. She lived in this house. She'd seen Brian in action. She knew it was wise to be afraid.

Mina scrambled back. "No, no, no, no, no, no." She couldn't stop the word from tumbling out of her mouth over and over, until the panic attack hit in full force, and her breathing escalated to the point that words couldn't come out at all. She was breathing too fast. The room was spinning. She felt dizzy.

She heard a door slam, but she was too lost inside herself to think about anything but the fact that she couldn't breathe right.

She jerked back when Brian invaded her physical space a few moments later. She recoiled at the sound of a snap. Her vision had narrowed in the panic, but she could barely make out a brown paper bag.

"Breathe into this."

Her hands shook as she took the bag from him and tried to do what he said to make it all stop.

His hand was steady and surprisingly gentle on her back, his words soothing instead of harsh. "Slowly in. Now out. Good. Again."

She breathed into the bag until she felt she could maintain the steady rhythm on her own.

She flinched when his fingers trailed gently through her hair. The way he touched her was a complete contradiction to his reputation. And she knew his reputation wasn't just stories. Every single person in the house reacted to him in such a way as to give credence to any story that spread about him.

Their previous encounters he'd been gentle as well. He'd helped her up when she'd fallen the first night. And then in the dungeon corridor, the way he'd touched her back and pressed his cheek against hers . . . He'd held her arms over her head, but he hadn't hurt her. He hadn't been rough or violent.

The opening of Chopin's *Nocturne 2* began to play on the CD player. She wasn't a classical music buff. She just knew what it was because she'd listened to it so many times on the discs Lindsay had given her. It was a famous piece, she'd just never known the name. It had been familiar. Safe.

On the CD, The pianist had played as if the music surprised him, or as if he were creating the piece himself in the moment. It felt unplanned. For some reason every time Mina listened to it, it made her cry. And yet she'd kept playing it.

She cried now as the piano played and Brian sat again beside her.

"The music . . . when I was going through withdrawal . . . it was from you?"

"It was. I sat outside your door. I didn't want to scare you."

His voice remained quiet and soothing but Jason had done the same in the beginning. Jason had seemed so reasonable. He'd magnanimously given her a safeword. And then he'd ignored it when she used it. There was no safeword with Brian. There was no point in pretending they were playing a game.

"D-did you buy me or did Lindsay just give me to you?"

Somehow it would be less of a betrayal if big money had actually exchanged hands. Though if he was just going to sell her to Brian, she didn't understand why he'd put her through all the drama in the medical room.

"Bought."

"H-how much?"

"That's none of your business."

She tensed and was quiet for several minutes, afraid she'd crossed a line already and was about to see first hand exactly how he'd acquired his reputation.

"Keep talking," he said, brushing a long strand of hair behind her ear. "I know that's not all that's troubling you. You will keep no secrets from me. Do you understand?"

"Y-yes, Master."

"Well?"

"W-why did you buy me?" This time she felt him tense beside her.

"The why isn't important. Just know I will honor the contract. I won't hurt you or cross the boundaries laid out. You will trust my word on that eventually. I have . . . other outlets."

The other girls here—the ones he would fuck and beat in Mina's place. She felt sickened that she had a split second of relief that maybe he could and would protect her as long as he had others to hurt instead. That thought should have produced revulsion, not relief. How would she stand to let him touch her, knowing the things he did to others and would continue to do?

"How will I trust that? I-I've heard about the things you do. And I can tell from looking in your eyes that you like it. You told me to run. And then the threats when I was in that cage . . ."

He rubbed her back, and the part of her that was in complete panic overload just wanted to rest and lean into him. It was crazier than any faith she'd put in the other men who had failed her, but all she wanted was something to hold onto, even if it wasn't real. If she could just pretend for a while and delay the inevitable.

"I told you to run because I didn't trust myself yet. But the man they were going to sell you to . . . I couldn't let them. I knew you wouldn't be safe."

"Why would you care?" This didn't match anything she'd heard about him. He should be gleeful at the idea of her suffering.

She wanted to believe this alternate reality in which she had some special power that not only kept her safe from Brian but shielded her from all outside harm under his protective wing. But how could she believe or trust that out of all the women in this house she was the sole one who was truly safe from him? That he wouldn't turn on her later? If he hadn't trusted himself near her only a week ago, what had changed in that time?

"Just know that I do care, and you will not be harmed. I don't want you to fear me."

"But the threats . . ."

"I didn't want you in the cage."

"But why?"

"That's enough. We're done discussing this."

Already he seemed to exist in that schizophrenic place she'd seen so many dominants in. That place of "You will tell me everything. No, shut up." It had been a favorite ploy of Jason's. She was beginning to think these men believed their own bullshit when they said they wanted no secrets, that they wanted to know everything. But they only wanted to know the things that kept their own fantasies going, not anything that might be real or true.

The intercom on the wall buzzed. "I'm sorry to interrupt, but we have a behavioral problem for you to deal with. A fight broke out at the pool," Lindsay said.

Brian sighed. "Who?"

"A new girl."

"Put her in cell B. It's set up and ready to go."

Brian turned back to Mina like a hawk sizing up prey. He went to a drawer and took out a sweater, sweatpants and socks, and placed them on the bed beside her. Then he handed her some tennis shoes. "I think these are about your size. The other stuff is mine, so it'll be big. You can roam freely around the grounds while I'm occupied. I'll send a signal to the bracelet when I'm ready for you. Did Lindsay explain about the beeping?"

"H-he said if it beeped to go to his office."

"Well, now if it beeps you come down here to me."

"Y-yes, Master."

"Good. No one else is to touch you. If they do, you tell them I said no. They won't test it. You will call all the trainers, including the doctor, by their first names from now on. None of them have any authority over you. You are just like Annette now. Talk to her. She'll help you understand how you fit in."

Mina fought not to scramble away from him as he stroked her cheek.

"We'll get better acquainted soon."

Six

Brian resented being called away from her. He'd just gotten her. Waiting the week while the collar was made had almost driven him insane. It had taken all his willpower to stay away during that time. Each of their interactions only scared her more, and part of that was his fault. Maybe all of it was his fault.

It had seemed best to avoid causing her more panic. It would only be harder to undo the damage later. He still couldn't believe he'd let Lindsay practically clean out his bank account. But he'd never been in this for the money. They let him feed the beast here. He could satisfy the thing that wouldn't let him sleep. That was worth far more than wealth.

Maybe it was better this way.

The doctor had acted nonchalant over the intercom, but none of them seemed to care much for Brian's methods. If they were calling him in, what had transpired upstairs must have been spectacular.

He should get this urge out of his system before trying to engage with Mina. It would give her time to process, maybe make peace with things.

But if the look in her eyes was any indication, she'd never make peace with things. And why should she? She knew he was a monster.

The look she'd given him was a mixture of terror and revulsion. On anyone else it hadn't bothered him. He didn't care if any of the others lived or died. But from her . . . it hurt—even though he'd expected the reaction.

He shook those thoughts away as he opened the door to cell B. He hadn't believed this would be a fairy tale. Mina would obey him, he was sure of it. She was too afraid not to. But she wouldn't love him. She wouldn't care for him. There wasn't a soul living who could be expected to take on such a task. He didn't require her body or her soul. Even her obedience was somewhat incidental. He just needed her near. He needed her safe. He just needed to know that at least one of them was okay and not being tormented and abused. If she could be okay, maybe he could somehow absorb that energy and keep the nightmares locked away forever.

Brian pulled a rolling metal cart in front of an iron chair. There were straps at the arms and the two front legs. The other partners set a limit on how much Brian could mark them, though occasionally he got carried away. But he could at least scare the shit out of them.

He laid out a fresh white paper sheet on the metal cart, then began to carefully place the sterilized tools on it. Some looked medical. Some looked like standard horror movie torture fare. He couldn't do anything that would damage the merchandise too much. And what marks he did leave would be intensely cared for upstairs in the infirmary so as to ensure the best healing. But when Brian punished, he did it right the first goddamn time.

Only one girl in the house had failed to succumb to him: Sabrina, former house brat and social queen bee. She'd somehow wormed her way in with Anton and gained his protection from Brian—a strategy increasing numbers of girls had tried since then as the rumors had drifted down. In the end, Anton's mercy cost the girl everything. She'd been disposed of. She was a liability. And a disruption. Ever since, any signs of rebellion or the girls organizing behind this or that brat leader were dealt with swiftly to spare them similar fates.

Brian's eyes lit when Lindsay brought his new toy in. He'd only seen her once or twice in passing and hadn't paid her much mind. Though he often pushed many of the girls in the gym and got to zap them a few times on their bracelet with the remote when they were too slow or lazy or whining, a lot of them never saw the inside of his dungeons. The stories were enough to keep them docile.

Lindsay threw the girl down on the ground and tossed a phone to Brian. It was the video footage of what she was being punished for.

"Close the door behind you," Brian said. "And lock it." He had his own key, and he didn't want this fresh new find—who was just becoming aware of the danger she was in—to get the opportunity to flee.

When the door shut and the lock turned over, he smiled.

"And what is your name, sweetheart?"

"Jessa, Sir."

"Jessa," he repeated. He hadn't even had this one in the gym. This was the first time they'd spoken. What a treat for their first time to be down here. This room was a place where lifelong bonds were formed. Desperate alliances between captive and captor.

"And how long have you been with us?"

"T-two days."

She was already crying. Delicious. Two days. She'd barely had a chance to take in the sights. She probably hadn't yet fucked half the men she would fuck in this house before her time came to be sold. It was practically like deflowering a virgin.

"Come here."

She crawled to him and pressed her lips against his boot. "P-please. I'm sorry."

"I'm sure you will be."

Brian strapped her into the chair while she blubbered and begged, then he pulled up a rolling leather chair and sat to watch the surveillance footage on Anton's phone.

He let out a low whistle as he watched the trembling girl in front of him hold another girl underwater in the pool. Jessa wasn't just fighting. She wanted to murder the girl. He knew that determination and hatred. It took three guys to get Jessa off of the victim and get them both out of the pool.

"Ordinarily I wouldn't care, but I'm in a good mood today so I'll indulge you . . . what did she do to you?"

"She called me a cunt."

They were right. She needed swift discipline or she'd be another Sabrina, bringing the whole house down while she got away with murder. Maybe literally.

Brian rolled his chair closer to his captive and placed the phone next to the tools. He picked up a gleaming, sharp knife. He couldn't actually use it on her today, but she didn't know that. And even after only two days in the house, he was sure the name Brian had passed in hushed tones through somebody's lips.

He dragged the blade against her arm, then raised it so that the point pricked and drew the smallest drop of blood. "We can't have behavior like that in this house."

"P-please don't. Please." Her eyes were wide as they took in the various instruments on the cart, convinced he was about to use them all on her.

Oh, if only.

He knew she wanted to ask what some were, but she was smart not to call attention to them. At least she wasn't as idiotic as she'd seemed in that video.

Brian put the knife back down. Jessa let out a sigh of relief until he picked up a syringe.

"W-what is that?"

A malicious smile spread across his face as he picked the knife up, ripped through the sarong that covered her legs, and grabbed a tawse from the second shelf of the cart. He rapped her leg hard, leaving a welt. "What is that SIR?" he snarled.

"W-what is that, Sir?"

"Better. It's my own blend. I could have been a chemist if I wasn't so fucked-up." It had been his major in college. And the truth was, he would have been far better off surrounded by arcane chemical compounds in glass beakers than by people.

"W-what will it do, Sir?"

She looked like she might pass out. He was going to have to pace himself here.

He shrugged. "Let's find out."

The contents of the syringe were relatively safe. It wasn't wise to inject random things into the bloodstream, but this wouldn't harm her—though she had no way of knowing that. And it was going to burn like a son of a bitch.

She strained against the straps as the needle came closer. Then it was as if she didn't know what to do with herself. Beg for mercy? Cry? Scream? She opted for all three.

Brian put a hand over her mouth. Her breathing still came loud and panicked even with muffling. He put the syringe down and moved even closer.

"Maybe I could be persuaded to do other things instead of hurting you." He slipped a hand between her legs. "Would you prefer that?"

She nodded vigorously as he pulled his hand away from her mouth.

"Yes, Sir. Please. I promise I won't cause any more trouble."

He leaned in and licked, then bit the side of her neck. Her body arched closer to him, desperate to appease. Poor little thing. There wasn't much she could do to attempt to seduce him when he had her strapped down like this.

Brian turned her face to his and forced a kiss from her. Because it was her first time here and she didn't know enough to know that this wouldn't work at all on him, she leaned into it and gave him all the passion she had to give in that kiss. He took, and she gave with even more fervor.

For such a rebel with such laughable self-control, she was ready to capitulate quickly. He hadn't even *started* on her yet—not a single mark except for that tiny prick from the point of the knife. But the mind fuck . . . that was where the real show was.

He picked up the syringe. "Now, where were we?"

He made a show of dabbing her arm with an alcohol swab and searching for the vein while she squirmed and struggled.

"If you aren't still, it's going to hurt a lot more, and it's going to bruise. Do you want that?"

She shook her head. "Please, I'll do anything you want."

She was offering sex in her artless way—most likely a blow job, and she was just still so new here she couldn't bring herself to say the words. How delightfully precious.

"Oh, you'll do that anyway."

He plunged the needle into her arm, and she screamed loud enough to wake a slumbering army. Brian breathed in deeply as if savoring the opening strains of a symphony.

Mina was grateful that she didn't have to go upstairs to face everyone in nothing but lingerie. He didn't have to give her dignity. He could have made her parade around naked if he'd wanted. Being dressed warmly also meant she could get out of the house to try to clear her head.

The pool was connected to the house, surrounded by high glass walls. Outside, snow drifted onto the glass, melting as it hit. The trees and ground were covered in a white peaceful blanket that didn't at all match the turmoil inside her.

She couldn't stop thinking about what Brian might be doing downstairs with that girl. She wasn't worried he might have sex with her. It wasn't as if Mina loved him. And even if she ever could, if he'd turn that attention on someone else, maybe that was better.

Annette sat next to a trembling woman near the pool. Something dramatic had obviously just happened. She looked up when she saw Mina.

"Are you okay?" she mouthed silently.

Mina shook her head. Annette left the girl beside the pool and joined her. Other girls had gathered, whispering and sending furtive glances Mina's way.

"Do they know?"

"That Brian bought you?" Annette asked. "They know. They watched him carry you out of the showroom."

A girl Mina had never spoken to, sauntered up. She'd been skinny dipping and didn't have an ounce of self-consciousness about her state of undress. "Owned by the sadistic psycho of the house. It couldn't have happened to a more deserving person."

They'd all known about her lack of training and had been irritated that she'd been given *special privileges.*

"I see they finally gave up on protecting you from him. I wonder how much money it took for them not to care what the hell happened to you."

"Shut up, Bree," Annette said. It was meant as a dismissal but the girl just kept talking.

She smiled icily, keeping her eyes on Mina. "I'm looking forward to this show. I can't wait to see how badly he fucks you up. I wonder if the scars will be visible or if they'll all just be psychological. Good thing we have a free shrink on the premises. You'll need him."

Annette pushed Bree into the pool. "Ooops."

"You cunt!" she screeched, when she surfaced.

"Careful, someone nearly got drowned for that not fifteen minutes ago. And remember, Brian can't touch *me.*"

If only Mina could be so lucky.

Annette looped an arm in Mina's and steered her from the group. She'd seen Annette around the house, though they hadn't spoken. Right now she behaved as if they were best friends—something Mina found solace in.

"I have to escape," Mina whispered when they stepped outside into the snow.

Annette shook her head and signaled for her to be quiet. Mina glanced around, wondering if there was surveillance that might catch her words. She'd thought being outside that it was okay, but they were still close to the house. There were hedges back here. Listening devices could easily be hidden. Either Annette knew of such devices, or she suspected.

Mina followed Annette through the yard until it seemed they were going off the property.

She jerked her arm back. "I can't. I'll get zapped."

"This is still safe. I know where all the property lines are." Of course she did.

They walked for what felt like forever before Annette finally stopped in the woods.

"The electric fence ends just before you get to the tree line in most places, but here, you can go into the woods for a bit."

"How do you know how far?"

"I marked the tree." She pointed at a tree a distance off with white paint on it. In the snow it was barely discernible. They stopped just before the painted tree.

"This is far outside the range of their spying equipment. Sometimes when I need to think and have some peace and freedom, I come out here. You're the first person I've brought here. I thought you might need a place like this, too."

"Do you ever think of escaping?"

Annette shook her head. "No. I'm happy here. I love Anton. He's good to me. And who wouldn't want to live in a place like this? Plus, it's not like I never get to leave. He takes me to the ballet and the opera. He's got friends from St. Petersburg in the ballet."

Perhaps off of Mina's desolate expression, Annette stopped herself and said, "Uh, but, I mean . . . I understand why you'd want to leave. If our situations were reversed . . ." she trailed off. "I'm sorry this happened to you."

"Help me find a way out. I can't be here. Not with him." She braced herself against the tree while she fought to keep her breath. There were no paper bags out here to stop it if she hyperventilated again. She felt unsteady on her feet, the cold woods spinning around her.

"Whoa. You need to sit somewhere," Annette said.

Mina leaned against the tree and tried not to think.

"Do they know you know about this place? Do they know this is inside the perimeter?"

"I have no idea. Anton's never said anything."

"What if I run through the barrier and just kept going? What if I pushed through far enough to get out of range?"

"It wouldn't work. The range of the fence is far enough that you wouldn't be able to withstand it. You'd go unconscious and they'd find you, assuming you survived that long."

"What about a key?"

"It's a code. They all know it by heart. It's not written down anywhere, and I've never been allowed close enough to see one come off."

Mina felt the tears begin to freeze on her face. "There has to be a way out. I . . . I can't go back." She recalled the look on Brian's face when he'd had her alone inside his room before he'd been called away. Something terrible would have happened if the intercom hadn't come on.

Even if he managed self-control today . . . what about tomorrow? Or the next day? Or the next? Eventually he'd hurt her. Badly.

Mina tugged on the bracelet as if it would come apart if she pulled on it the right way.

"You should talk to Lindsay."

"He won't do anything," Mina said, defeated.

"Well, you'd better figure out a way to appeal to him. He's your only shot. He brought you here. He accepted Brian's bid—at least that's what Anton said. The others stayed out of it. Lindsay is the only one with the power to set you free. Well, except for Brian, but I doubt that will happen. Just go talk to him."

Loud beeps went off, causing Mina to jump, convinced it was Brian calling her back, but it wasn't her bracelet.

"That's Anton. I have to go. Remember what I said. If you want out, you have to work on Lindsay."

It was Sunday, so Lindsay was at the house, instead of at his office in the city.

"What is it?" he said when she knocked.

She pushed the door open a crack and popped her head in.

"Mina." His voice held resignation. "Come in, and close the door."

Seething rage curled off her. He'd betrayed her. If she hadn't been so disoriented when Brian released her to wander, she would have come straight to the doctor and screamed at him for being such a fucking liar.

"Lindsay, I hate you. You are fucking filth for doing this to me, and I will never forgive you as long as I live."

It wasn't the way out of here, but she'd already begged and pleaded for him to keep her himself, and that had fallen on deaf ears. Not that she wanted to be his anymore after the myriad ways he'd hurt her. She'd already asked to be released. The answer had been no. There was no reason to think his decision would change now.

He reeled back as if she'd hit him. It took him a moment to gain his composure, and then his expression hardened. She knew now that his civilized facade was perhaps the weakest in the house. Even Brian had managed not to yell at her yet.

"Sir," he gritted out.

"No." At least with her master's order, Brian was the only one who could do anything to her. Not that that was much comfort.

"I'm sorry . . . No?"

"Brian said not to give anyone else any formal address and that no one here has any authority over me but him."

"Dr. Smith, then," he said after a long, disgruntled moment.

"No. He said first names only." She watched as the doctor struggled to push the rage down.

"Very well, then."

"You lied to me. You said you would sell me to someone kind. You said I would be happy and safe. And then you give me to the biggest psycho you know?"

"He swore he'd honor the contract."

"And you *believed* him?" Wasn't Lindsay supposed to have some vague understanding of human behavior? Was he even licensed? Did he have a real degree?

"Has he hurt you?"

"He hasn't had time yet. He was called away. But there's nothing to stop him."

"I know this is hard to understand and accept right now, but I believe he needs you. I believe he truly means you no harm. Just try to take a step back. Take a moment to think about what sorts of things might make a person become like Brian."

"What are you trying to say?"

He shrugged. "That's the point. I can't say. He's spoken to me in confidence. I can schedule an appointment to check in with you daily to ensure you are safe if it will make you feel better."

"And what if I'm not?" There was silence while the doctor looked down at his hands. "You know you can't stop him. You just gave me to a sadist because he gave you enough money to sooth your conscience."

"Mina, that's not . . ."

"I don't want to hear it." She got up and slammed the door on her way out. Her situation may be terrible, but at least she didn't have to kiss the doctor's ass anymore. Or his boots. Fuck him. Fuck all of them. She wanted to include Brian in that big fat fuck-you, but he hadn't hurt her. Yet.

Mina climbed the endless steps to the tower. She doubted anybody would send her things. If she wanted them, it would be up to her to move them.

She packed her bags, trying not to think about where she was taking them. She caught her reflection in the mirror and stared at the collar.

She'd forgotten it was around her throat. There had been too much panic to give it a second thought beyond her initial reaction. But now that she knew who it was from . . . What did that mean? He'd noticed her ring and taken the time to have a collar made to match it. And what about the Chopin? And how he'd made the exchange as easy for her as he could? And all the small moments she'd shared with him. None of it went with the picture of Brian she'd been given, or her strong instincts to avoid him.

Mina shook the thoughts from her head. No. She'd been down this road. She'd played these games. It was the same bullshit small kindnesses to make her rational-ize away her smarter instincts—if she had any at all.

She lugged her suitcases down the many flights of stairs, ignoring the gawking from the girls in the house as she passed.

When she got the luggage to the dungeon corridor, she paused to catch her breath. And in that pause, she heard the screams coming from cell B.

She couldn't stop herself from going to the door where the sounds emitted. The cell had a window, and Mina didn't have the strength of will not to sate her curiosity. Upon looking, she wished she'd resisted the temptation. What had she hoped to see that could possibly make her feel any better?

The woman was nude and tied to a pole in the center of the room. Her arms were crossed and tied over her head, and then farther down, her waist had been tied to keep her in place, allowing Brian to nudge her legs apart. Harsh marks glared from where he'd whipped her, and her face was swollen from crying. He fucked her, one hand wrapped around her throat, pulling her back closer.

"Tell me what you love to be called now?" he growled.

"Cunt," she whimpered.

"So, if someone else calls you that again, it won't be a problem, will it?"

"N-no, Sir."

Whatever awful things he'd done to her—and there was plenty of evidence that it had been bad, from the marks he'd left all the way to the implements that lay strewn around the cell as if just used—somehow, against all odds, she'd succumbed to him and the pleasure he took from her.

He looked up, and his eyes met Mina's. His stare was hard. He thrust into the woman harder, a defiant look on his face as if he dared Mina to be jealous or complain or even feel sorry for her.

Mina turned and fled back up the stairs. She ran on pure adrenalin. Her mind raced as she tried to determine a place to hide—a place he wouldn't find her. As if that existed.

There was nowhere to go, but if she found a good enough hidden nook in this vast labyrinth of rooms, surely he'd leave her alone for a while.

She rejected spot after spot until she found the library. The library took up a large portion of the east wing of the house and stood two stories. The space was immense and deserted. On the second floor were rows and rows of boring reference books that seemed to only exist because no quality library would be without them. Tucked away in the back was a storage room. It seemed to have been forgotten, nearly concealed behind a bookshelf and some dilapidated furniture.

Given the dust, it didn't look as if anyone had been there for some time. The beeping started. Brian was calling. She tried to ignore it, but the sound was unrelenting. She took a pillow from the old couch and covered it to muffle the beep.

She was relieved when the sound muted. But what if the beeping never stopped? How would she ever leave this spot? She'd have to use the bathroom and eat at some point. With the security band screaming like a car alarm, it wasn't as if she could move through the house without notice.

After about twenty minutes, the noise subsided. Had he given up? Had the beeping simply run its course?

All at once, the stress of the day caught up to her. She curled up in the corner and slept.

Seven

Mina felt strong arms around her. She was being carried. Without opening her eyes she knew it was Brian. She already knew the feel of him, the smell of him, the aura of shadows and pain that surrounded him. It was the foreboding feeling one got immediately upon waking from a nightmare—only she'd never wake from Brian.

"There's a tracking device inside your collar. There is nowhere you can go to hide from me. I knew where you were when I activated the beeper. I just wanted to see if you would come to me on your own. Now I have my answer."

He was too calm, as if he'd laid out some horrible punishment, and the thought of it kept him appeased. She struggled and squirmed, but he held her tighter. She screamed.

Lindsay rushed out of his room, naked, with a woman in an equal state of dress clinging to him. The doctor extracted himself from the woman's grip and followed them.

"Brian!"

Her master stopped. "What!" he growled.

"Mina, are you all right?"

"Oh she's peachy. Don't you know the sound of a scream of delight when you hear one? Oh, no, I guess you don't."

The doctor glared. "Just let me talk to her in my office. Perhaps I should speak with you as well."

Brian's nostrils flared. "Absofuckinglutely not! No! You will not get in the middle of this—analyzing and making notes about us. You are done seeing me, and from now on you are done seeing Mina. No more digging in either of our heads. I don't want you in the middle between us!"

In the midst of his tirade, he set Mina on her feet so he could more effectively invade Lindsay's personal space. She gripped the wall to steady herself, contemplating running—not that she'd get far. Between the electronic bracelet and the tracking device in her collar, escaping him even for a short while was futile. And enraging him more wasn't on her top list of things to do right now.

Brian slammed Lindsay against the wall, and the naked girl fled into the doctor's bedroom. "No more fucking head shrinking! No more games and notes and psychoanalysis bullshit. She is MINE! Do you understand me? Do you?"

"B-Brian, I promised her. I swore to her that I would keep seeing her, that I would check in with her and make sure she was okay."

"And if she wasn't? Who would you send as enforcer? How would you protect her from me, you fool?"

"You said you wouldn't harm her."

"And have I? Have I harmed her? Have I laid a finger on her?" Brian rounded on Mina, and she shrank back.

"Tell the good doctor here. Have I hurt you? Beat you? Raped you? Anything horrific?"

How could she answer such a question? She'd literally been alone with him five minutes before he'd been called away to torture some poor girl. And the way he was behaving now didn't show much promise.

"N-no, Master," she stammered, even though what she wanted to say was, "Not yet." A tremble spread through her limbs, and she couldn't stop it.

"She's terrified of you," Lindsay said.

"She was terrified of me from the moment she first laid eyes on me. So nothing's changed," Brian retorted.

"Please listen to reason. It will go so much easier if you'll just let me treat her. And you, too. We can make this work."

"No! Do not interfere with us, or you will beg me for death by the time I'm finished with you. Are we clear?"

Lindsay nodded quickly, and Brian backed off. He grabbed Mina's hand and dragged her to the main level, past curious stares, and down to the dungeons.

Once inside his room he shoved her onto the bed. The anger rose off him, threatening to materialize and strangle the breath from her.

"I'm going to take a shower. You'd better still be here when I get back."

He slammed the bathroom door, and a few moments later the water began to run. The betrayal swamped her. Now more than ever she needed to know how much money it had taken for the doctor to pretend this was okay. She believed Brian would kill Lindsay if he didn't stay away, and a dark part of her felt satisfied at the thought. Because this was the man who'd subjected her to Brian, the one person in this house she'd prayed to safely avoid until she left this place.

Brian's room wasn't much different than many of the other rooms at the house. There were shackles on the wall above the bed, but that was no different than her tower room. A fireplace stood against one wall, making the space feel almost cozy.

It was only the fact that it was underground and its close proximity to the dungeons that made the room feel malevolent and remote.

Besides the bathroom and the closets, there was another door she hadn't noticed. It was locked with no window or peep hole to see what was behind it. Just a locked door.

She sat on the bed and hugged her knees to her chest and watched the black clock on the wall. Fifteen minutes passed. Any moment he would come out of that bathroom and whatever horrible thing he had planned for her would begin in earnest. But then another fifteen minutes passed and no Brian. The water kept running.

It was a long time to take a shower. She got off the bed and moved closer to the door. Had something happened to him? God, she hoped so. Please let her be lucky enough for him to have stroked out or had a heart attack right there in the bathroom. Please. Please.

But when she pushed the door open, she heard crying. No, it wasn't crying. This was deeper and more profound. This was gut wrenching sobbing—the kind of grief expressed when the love of your life dies.

As she stepped inside, the sobbing stopped. But he didn't turn around. The anger and fight seemed to have deflated out of him. At least for now. Brian sat in the glassed-in shower, his knees drawn to his chest, his back to her. The water must be freezing by now.

Something drove her on, pushing her closer, despite the clear danger he posed to her—the danger he posed to all living things. She let out an audible gasp when she saw his back. It was striped with scars as bad as hers. A few perhaps worse. Who could have ever done something like this to him?

The scars were old and stretched. That was when she realized. He'd only been a child. Growth spurts had stretched the scars, making them appear even more grisly than they might have, had they been created on a grown man.

Was this why he was the way he was?

The fear and instincts to fear fell away, and everything seemed to crystallize in front of her bright and clear like the answers to the universal questions had been elegantly written out for her in the drops of water still coming from the shower. It wasn't about her anymore. All she felt in that moment was compassion. This was nothing like Jason. This was something different.

Brian heard the door creak as she slipped in—then her gasp when she noticed the mangled scars on his back. If another person had seen him like this, they would've been met with swift violence, but not Mina.

He'd spent the last half hour mentally berating himself for yelling in front of her. It hadn't been aimed at her. He'd only been goading the doctor. The gall of Lindsay to think he could insinuate himself between them, that he could micromanage the relationship and keep his nose pressed against the glass recording and documenting everything. Never. Lindsay had no place or business here.

Still, he'd shouted in her direction. He'd lost control in front of her, and now she was even more afraid of him if that were possible.

He jumped when the shower door opened, and a moment later her warm hand was on his shoulder. He covered it with his own, and they stayed like that for a long time.

"The water's cold," she said.

"Yeah."

She reached with her free hand and turned it off. The last bit of icy water gurgled as it slid down the drain.

"Go back to the bedroom, undress, and get in the bed. I'll be there in a minute." It was only early evening, but he was so tired, like every last ounce of energy and life had drained from him. It had been a long day. It had been a long week waiting for her. He just needed time to prove that whatever kind of monster he was, she didn't ping his radar the same way.

Her hand tensed underneath his but she went without a word.

When the door clicked shut, he struggled to stand and grabbed a towel from the rack. He shivered when the cool air hit him. It was so weak for him to be in here crying like this, like a baby. Like the child he'd once been. When would it stop chasing him?

She won't tell anyone.

Even if he permitted her to see the doctor, she wouldn't tell. He'd felt it in the energy that had passed between them. She was his in a way that went beyond collars and captivity or any amount of money. She didn't know it yet, but he'd felt it just now when she'd left a piece of her soul in his hands.

Brian gripped the sink, steeling himself against the emotions that still overwhelmed him. He'd been hurt that she'd hidden and ignored his call. But what had he expected? She didn't know yet that he was her protector.

It made him feel powerful in a new way . . . instead of breaking things, holding them together. The itchy darkness that slithered under his skin was quiet and still. For now. He held no illusions that it was over, that somehow she'd saved him and pulled his soul from the brink. It wasn't like that. The monster would call for someone else's blood and tears, but now it demanded something more, something he'd never given to another soul and wasn't sure he had the ability to give.

When he stepped out of the bathroom he felt her fear, and unlike the other women, it made a sick feeling knot inside his stomach because when he saw her afraid like that, all he could see was himself. Until this point in his history, the normal reaction for someone taking him back to that place under the stairs would have been anger, violence. Any reaction to make it go away. But hurting her felt like hurting himself, and he'd been hurt enough for one lifetime already.

Mina's clothes were neatly folded in a nearby chair. She was under the covers, curled on her side facing the bathroom door. Wide, frightened eyes rose to his.

Brian took the towel from his waist and draped it over the chair with her clothes, then he joined her.

Her lip trembled, and she started to cry. Whatever bravery she'd managed to summon in the bathroom had abandoned her. She recoiled when he touched the side of her cheek.

"Shhhh. Roll onto your stomach."

She hesitated, but then seemed to fear inciting his wrath for the hesitation and rolled over as he'd asked. He pulled the covers back, and she cringed as the air hit her.

This was the first time he'd gotten a truly good, unfettered look at her back, at what those monsters had done to her.

Monsters like you? A voice in his mind whispered.

No. In all likelihood, the monsters that had gotten hold of her were nowhere near as bad as Brian was capable of being, which made it all the more ridiculous that he thought he would somehow be better for her.

But these marks, brutal though they were, were the marks of amateurs. Unbalanced, sociopathic amateurs, but amateurs all the same. They weren't made from the same anger and pain that had crafted Brian. They weren't retribution. They weren't solace. They were boredom and the basic thrill of lording power over another.

She shivered when he swept her dark hair out of the way. He trailed his fingers over each mark in turn as if he could erase them by touching them the right way. He kissed a languid path down her back. Her hands dug into the bed linens beside her.

"Relax, Mina. I will never hurt you. I have other kinds of toys for that." He wouldn't use a loaf of bread to hammer a nail. Why would he break something that belonged solely to him? Because she thought he was crazy. And he couldn't blame her, given their experiences together up to this point and the things she must have heard.

While waiting for her collar to be made, he'd worried that all the time she spent in the house would give her too many opportunities to learn things which would only make it that much harder for both of them when she knew who she belonged to.

At night, he'd stood in the shadows and watched her swim. She didn't have a swimsuit, so she'd gone naked. She'd been tentative and fearful at first, but when she didn't see him or anyone else, she'd lost the inhibition. She'd seemed free, and now he was afraid she might never be that way again.

He pushed those thoughts away. "Don't talk to Lindsay about us. I mean it. If you do, I'll find out about it."

She tensed under his hands. He didn't like scaring her. He didn't want to, but he needed her to keep her mouth shut around Lindsay. Letting him into their world was too invasive. He wouldn't live under the doctor's constant surveillance. Lindsay didn't get to impose himself into Anton and Annette's relationship. So why should he get to be a third party in Brian and Mina's?

"Do you understand?" he asked, knowing full well that she did. She wasn't a child. Still, he needed to know she'd heard the command. He felt certain that if she heard him explicitly forbid the action, she'd be too afraid to go against him.

"Yes, Master," she whispered.

Brian stretched out and pulled her unresisting body against him. "I'm very tired," he said. Or maybe he thought it. He wasn't sure if he got the words out before sleep claimed him.

Mina lay still as Brian's breath moved in and out in a steady rhythm against her skin. What just happened? After the display with Lindsay she was sure he'd lose control, that he'd hurt her—today. Not later.

The reality was quite different.

He hadn't even touched her sexually. Nor had he insisted she touch him. If not for how frightening he was, she would have been attracted. She found him almost painfully attractive. She would have been more than willing to touch him and let him touch her if she could trust he wouldn't hurt her like the others—if she could get past what he did to other women here.

He had the chiseled physique of a god, though it was more likely he was a gym rat with a level of dedication that hinted he had a touch of masochism to go with his sadism.

Even finding him sobbing in the bathroom hadn't diminished the feeling of threat. Nor had his scars put a damper on his good looks. In fact, once she'd gotten to the bedroom to carry out his order, she'd been terrified he was about to punish her for seeing that, for intruding on his moment of whatever pain he'd been working through, and for discovering that once upon a time, he'd been someone's cowering victim, too.

It was only eight-thirty. Her stomach growled. It had been a long day, and very little food had reached her. Brian's breath deepened.

In sleep he wasn't the intimidating presence he was while awake. There was no dark, intense staring to contend with. The angry lines of his face softened. The muscles of his body relaxed and melted into the bedding around him.

He hadn't bothered turning the light off when he'd emerged from the bathroom. She wondered if he'd intended to fall asleep. Before Mina could stop herself, she reached out to trace the scars along his back.

She'd clearly lost her mind. Who knew what he'd do if he woke to find her doing this? She doubted she'd ever know the story behind them. In the week waiting under the ruse that some party outside the house had bought her, she'd heard a lot of things about Brian—how he liked to hurt women. Girls upstairs said that whoever you displeased in this house, never let it be Brian. It had been impressed upon her that if she were to upset one of the others, the best outcome was to throw herself on their mercy and take whatever punishment they would mete out. Because if they outsourced it to Brian—it would be worse.

She'd heard he only fucked women from behind, he rarely took his shirt off to do it, and sometimes he blind-folded them. At the time it had been random boogeyman trivia. It was the kind of thing campers told around campfires—ghost stories meant to scare the shit out of you right before bed.

Now those tidbits came together and meant something. He didn't want them to see. Yet he'd already allowed Mina that close. He'd been vulnerable with her. She wanted it to mean something. She wanted it to confirm that somehow he could keep his promises—that at the very least he wanted to.

She kissed his back, careful not to wake him. She needed to know what it felt like to press her lips against his skin without coercion or fear. She wanted to experiment to see if she could handle it.

As she peppered kisses down his back, the reality proved more frightening than she'd expected. Because what she felt when she kissed him wasn't revulsion or disgust. Brian might be the one person who could understand her pain. Even if he got sick pleasure in meting it out to others, he could understand her in a way far more intimate than Lindsay.

She didn't know why she'd wanted Lindsay to begin with. The doctor would nod and say, "mmhmmm". He'd make notes and pretend he understood. But all he understood were clinical labels and pet psychological theories. He didn't *get it*. He knew how to file and label and categorize, but it was as if he were missing a major sense and merely faking what it must be like as he scribbled on the yellow legal pad.

Brian had known the moment their eyes met that first night. He'd known something more than the doctor would ever be privy to. And though she was afraid, she agreed with him. The doctor could never be allowed inside whatever this was. No matter how scary it was, how scary Brian was, there was the kernel of something inside him that felt like home and understanding. Like he'd lived on that street.

Brian slept on, oblivious. He slept deeply enough that if she wanted to, she could kill him. There was no one else in the house who had the potential to be as danger-ous to her as Brian.

There had to be a key somewhere in his room or clothing that would let her inside one of the dungeons. Those cells had weapons. But even as she thought it, a coldness rushed over her, as if the house itself read her thoughts and disapproved of them.

Wasn't this why she kept getting into such dangerous situations with men who hurt her? Because she ignored her instincts when they told her to run, because she stupidly kept walking into these situations hoping that *this one* wouldn't hurt her?

Couldn't she this one time do something smart and eliminate the threat before the threat eliminated her? But watching him sleep, his softened expression, the scars, she couldn't bring herself to end his life. Maybe he'd be like Jason. Maybe he'd be worse. And it didn't matter.

She was already forming that weird captive/captor alliance. If she couldn't slit his throat right now, she'd never be able to do it, no matter what he did. The clocked ticked loudly as the seconds lurched on.

Brian rolled over, his arm moving around her, pulling her closer. It was the final nail in the coffin of her unending foolishness. There was no one in the world anymore to blame but herself.

He whimpered in his sleep, and a tear rolled down his face. God, what had happened to him? She brushed the tear away and struggled to roll back over until they were cuddled together, his body wrapped around hers. It should have felt claustrophobic and stifling, but it didn't. He held onto her like she were life itself. After a few moments the awful sounds subsided, his breathing evened out again, and whatever had been chasing him in his dreams went away.

Mina's stomach growled again. She had to get upstairs before the kitchen closed. She eased out from under his arm until his grip loosened, then she got out of the bed and quietly dressed. She didn't bother with shoes. Despite all the stone work and the hard floors, the estate was kept well-heated, especially upstairs.

She held her breath as she opened the door, waiting for the creak to work itself out. She glanced back at him, but he slept on. She left before she lost her nerve again.

On the main floor, the atmosphere was very different. People milled about. Debauchery was at its peak. Girls who weren't otherwise occupied were making last minute runs on the cafeteria. It felt like a college dorm—so different from the cave downstairs that Brian lived in where no light seemed to ever touch him.

Lindsay stopped her in the entryway, concern in his eyes. *Now* he was concerned. After he'd brought her into this. After he'd threatened her with Brian. After he'd made good on that threat in the most final way possible.

"Are you all right? Has he hurt you?" He gripped her shoulders, searching her face, looking for outward signs of violence.

"Why do you care? You sold me to him." Even the idea galled her beyond all reason. Yes, she'd agreed to it, but that was when she still lived in a fantasy land and hadn't processed what she was signing on for.

Mina wasn't prepared to let this go. She doubted she'd ever forgive Lindsay for putting her in harm's way after she'd trusted him. Even if he was right. Even if Brian never laid a hand on her in anger, Lindsay hadn't known beyond all doubt that she'd be safe. And he hadn't had a true Plan B. That was made clear outside the doctor's room when her master had delivered his threats.

"Come to my office. Let's talk. Where is he?"

"I'm not allowed to talk to you about him or us." It wasn't just that she wasn't allowed to, she didn't want to. She both wanted to mentally torment the doctor for his poor decision-making and his greed, and she wanted to protect Brian. She shook that latter thought out quickly. That couldn't be right. Why? Why would she want that? No matter what had been done to him, he'd more than made up for it with viciousness of his own. So what the hell could he ever need protecting from? And did he even deserve it?

"I promise that whatever you say will remain between us. I won't say anything to him. No matter what he's told you or made you believe, he can't watch you every second. He can't know everything you do when he's not with you."

Who cared whether he could or not? And maybe he could. If there was a tracking device in her collar, couldn't there just as easily be a recording device? Brian wasn't stupid. He'd even seemed to know it was safe for him to sleep in her presence. Given whatever past he'd survived, he wouldn't have gone to sleep next to her if he hadn't been sure she wouldn't do anything.

Mina brushed past the doctor. "I said no. I have to get to the cafeteria before it closes."

He gripped her arm. Mina spun and slugged him in the jaw. She stared at her fist as she pulled it back. Her hand stung and would likely be bruised the next day.

He leaped back and held his jaw as a wounded puppy look came over his face.

Right. Because he was such a victim here. A moment later his mood changed, and his eyes flashed with rage. Why did they all fear Brian? Lindsay seemed to be the one with the hair trigger. At least with her. Maybe Jason was right. There was something inside her that made men want to hurt her.

"You think you can hit me?" He said. There it was. That entitled jackass dominant bullshit. Lindsay lunged for her and grabbed her wrist, forcing it behind her back as he pushed her face against the wall.

A group of girls gathered on the fringes to watch the drama unfold. The acoustics of the grand entryway made their whispers sound like loudly hissing serpents.

If she'd been operating only on instinct, she would have been afraid, but after Brian's display outside the doctor's room, she had no doubt that if he found out Lindsay laid a hand on her, she wouldn't be the one who had to fear anything.

"Let go of me and pray I don't tell him about this," she said.

Lindsay released her and stepped back, rattled. "I was trying to help you. I wanted to ensure you were safe, and this is how you repay me?"

He had her exit blocked, using sheer force of intimidation against her now that he realized the folly of touching her. Part of her hoped Brian would wake and come upstairs to see this, though she worried when he was finished with Lindsay, she'd have to pay for having left. But did he mean for her to starve? She'd barely eaten all day.

"You just want to soothe your guilty conscience. Get out of my way. I have to eat something."

"Fine, to hell with you then," Lindsay said. "Don't come crying to me later when he loses his shit on you."

"I wouldn't have to if you hadn't sold me to him in the first place! How much? How much did it take for you to just not give a shit about your promise to me?"

"five million," he whispered.

Mina heard a low whistle nearby. It made her want to punch someone.

"Dollars?" Because surely it couldn't be that. Rupees maybe, but not that many dollars.

Lindsay nodded. "He was insistent. He said he had to protect you from Matsumoto. That was the bidder who would have taken you. He said there was something not right about him."

She might have asked why Brian would have cared if not for seeing his back, the scars that so closely resembled her own. She knew why. She wasn't sure how, but the marks across her flesh made him see her differently—as someone not on the hurt list. For that she was grateful, even as she still worried he might lose control.

She pushed past the doctor.

"Are you going to tell him about this?" he asked, his voice low.

"I haven't decided." Maybe it wasn't just the scars that formed the kinship between Mina and Brian. With the smallest glimpse of power, she already saw how she might seek to abuse it. Had she been in Brian's position, she couldn't guarantee she wouldn't seek retribution in the way he had, and that thought scared her.

Mina managed to cover her distress and passed through the veil of whispers to get to the cafeteria line.

"Five minutes later, and you'd be going to bed without supper," an older woman said from behind the food counter.

Mina wondered how she'd come to be here and was convinced she was must be just as much a prisoner as Mina. Surely she'd tell someone what went on here if she were ever allowed to leave the premises.

"Everything?" the woman asked.

"Yes, please."

The woman behind the counter loaded roast, potatoes, and green beans onto the plate, and salad on another plate, then slid it to her. Mina took her tray to get some pie and a drink. Normally she wouldn't eat all this, but this was her only real meal today. She'd better make it count. And with the counter closing in a few minutes, she wouldn't be able to return for seconds.

A strange shift had happened. Before, she'd been taunted by the mean girls table, now they looked on curiously as if they were in the market for a new leader—or more likely, in the market to use somebody who might put in a good word of protection for them should Brian ever get them in his dungeon.

Annette sat across from her. "Is your hand okay?"

It still stung, but the skin wasn't broken. She'd probably done more damage to her own hand than she had to the doctor's jaw, but it felt liberating to fight back for the first time in perhaps ever.

Hitting the doctor, forcing him to back off—even if it had been the threat of who she belonged to and not any physical stopping power she had on her own—had accomplished what six months of therapy failed to. Maybe she should have taken up boxing instead.

Talking never had the hope of healing her. The only thing that would get her there was having control over her own life and having some power back. But that ship had sailed. If only she'd figured this out before she'd fallen for Lindsay's smooth talk and lies about only wanting what was best for her. Lindsay wanted what was best for Lindsay's bank account.

"Mina?"

"Sorry. Yeah, it's fine, I think. It might bruise. I don't know."

"Well, he deserved it. I still can't believe he sold you to Brian. Of all the sadistic shitheads to hand you over to."

Mina bristled at the insult to her master but didn't say anything. She wasn't prepared to admit that any part of her was already willing to defend him. The moment in the bathroom had shifted something inside her the tiniest amount.

She tried to ignore Anton's slave as she dug into her dinner. She'd been famished and was surprised she hadn't passed out.

"Are you okay? Has he hurt you?" Annette asked, echoing Lindsay's earlier pretend concern. From her the concern sounded convincing.

"I'm fine." For now.

Annette's eyes widened and Mina turned to see what had caught her attention. Brian stood in the middle of the cafeteria, watching her. Everyone else on the main level had given him a wide berth. He crossed the floor to Mina's table with a tray in his hands.

Annette got up as if her chair had been lit on fire and fled the area. Brian sat in the chair she'd vacated and started to eat his own dinner.

"I woke to find you gone," he said between bites. There was no inflection. No anger. Everything came out flat. The lack of emotion was perhaps more frightening than if there had been any.

"I'm sorry, Master."

"I haven't eaten much today, either."

Mina just stared at him. Never would she have expected someone with Brian's reputation to take anything she'd done calmly and rationally.

When he looked up, she switched her focus to her own food. She winced when he laid his hand over hers.

"What happened to your hand?"

Mina jerked it back. "N-nothing."

"Nothing, Master," he corrected. But he wasn't angry. Who was this guy? What had he done with the psycho?

"Nothing, Master," she repeated. But it didn't end the inquisition.

Instead, he grabbed her hand to inspect it. She didn't see any broken skin or enough redness to call attention to. He must have noticed her wince.

Brian pressed against the knuckles and watched her expression closely. "Does this hurt?"

"No, Master."

"Don't lie to me."

"A little."

"How did it happen?"

"She punched the doctor in the jaw!" one of the girls nearby, said.

Mina was sure the girl tattled on her because she thought Brian would hurt her. Information about her contract terms had leaked, and many in the house had decided she needed to be taken down a peg.

Lindsay seemed to appear out of a mist to stand beside the table. "Yes, she punched me in the jaw."

She couldn't determine if the doctor was trying to get her in trouble, too.

"I'm sure she had a good reason," Brian said.

He surely hadn't expected that response. Neither had Mina.

"Finish your dinner, and we'll go back downstairs," Brian said.

The two of them continued to eat in silence. After a few moments of being ignored, Lindsay wandered off.

When Mina finished, she picked up her tray to take it to the counter.

"Leave it. We have people for that."

He led her past the nosy bystanders and back down the stairs to their room. It was strange to hold Brian's hand like that, as if they were some young ordinary couple. Inside, he didn't immediately let go of her hand. Instead, he pulled her closer and held her against him. His warmth pushed through her clothes, through her skin, into her bones.

Finally he released her and sat in a chair across the room. "Undress."

Mina shivered.

"Are you cold?"

She nodded.

He flicked on the gas fireplace. It only took a few minutes for the room to turn toasty warm, warm enough that she wanted to take clothes off. He smirked from the chair as if he knew exactly what she was thinking.

"Strip," he said. "You have no more excuses."

He'd seen her already . . . kind of. This was no different. But it was. It was so different. For a moment she was back with Jason being passed around like some whore. Then she was in the medical room at the house, freezing

up, unable to do what was asked of her because she'd just
. . . hit the wall.

Now the wall rose again. What if she couldn't? What
if she said no? What would he do to her? She'd seen what
he *could* do. He could make whatever promises he
wanted—like the others had—but she'd seen his eyes
through the cell window when he'd been fucking that girl
he'd just beaten. Mina's breathing went shallow again,
and the room started to spin.

"Mina." His voice rolled over her like thunder in the
distance.

The tremble started in her lip, and she felt the tears
and the panic ready to explode out of her. How had she
ever thought she could do this again?

He motioned, and she went to him. He took both of
her hands in his and looked up. His expression reflected
her own pain—like he understood. "It's okay. I just want
to look at you. It will be okay. Give me this."

She wanted to.

"I saw you in the cage. And in the bed. This is just . . .
a little more."

She couldn't believe he was being so patient . . .
Brian. It gave her the strength to take her clothes off for
him.

"Turn away," he said when she was exposed and bare
before him.

He stood behind her and stroked her throat as he
pulled her against him. Then he began kissing her neck.
His mouth was so warm and soft against her skin that a
whimper slipped through her lips. Despite how he'd been
with her, she never could have imagined that his mouth
on her could feel like this—a shocking tenderness that
eviscerated her.

His other hand moved between her legs to stroke her most sensitive flesh. She found herself grinding against his fingers, forgetting whose arms she was in. It was impossible that Brian could touch someone so carefully. He must be the only person who could make methodical touch seem sensual. She worried he'd cross the boundaries laid out in her contract, but a part of her didn't care as long as he didn't hurt her. She had no illusions he'd honor the contract forever but held hope he wouldn't lose control and start beating her or passing her around to the other men at the house.

She whimpered again as his fingers flicked over her swollen bud. He chuckled as she bucked harder against him. It was a desperate searching for life, for love, for meaning, for any bright spark in the darkness of being his. He kept up his onslaught until she came apart in his arms.

"Get in bed."

She could barely make herself move in that direction half from the orgasm and half from fear of how he might now ruin it.

He removed his own clothing and joined her. "Let's talk about the contract I signed."

Here it was. How would he justify breaking it? How was he planning to wheedle around it. Perhaps now that it was clear Lindsay had no power to stop him, he'd outright flaunt it.

"The no-pain part, I understand. A lot of people don't like pain—probably what one might consider the *normal people*. But explain the penetration restriction. Were you sexually abused?"

He tried to sound nonchalant, but his jaw was clenched, and his hands fisted in the sheets.

"N-no, Master. I mean . . . yes, Jason and others . . . there was abuse, but even before all that, I never really liked . . . I mean . . . I told Lindsay in our sessions that I could handle it if I had to . . . but . . ."

"Okay. Let's define it then. More specifically."

Why was he doing this? Was it just so he could use it to hurt her later when he got pissed off? It felt like she was giving him the tools to hurt her with. As if he needed more of those.

"Blow jobs?"

"T-that's okay." She hadn't been thinking specifically in those terms when she'd told the doctor her limits. Or maybe she had. After all, hadn't she thought she might end up with someone gross? Brian was definitely not that.

"Okay. Anal sex or anal play?"

"N-no." She held her breath as if he'd become giddy, knowing something he could use to terrorize her.

"Okay. Fingers and toys? Inside you, I mean."

"I-I think okay." That was technically penetration. She hadn't been thinking about all the options when she'd struck the deal with Lindsay. And she hadn't believed anybody would give a shit about her limits. No one else had. It had been a way to safeguard and protect herself mentally. If she set impossible standards, when they were broken, she'd get the disappointment over with early and be able to steel herself for whatever came next.

"So no anal anything and no standard intercourse?"

She nodded.

"I can work around that."

But why would he? Why would he care what she wanted at all? He'd paid a large sum of money for her, more than she could even visualize. She was his property, his prisoner. He was a sadist. What difference could it possibly make what she wanted?

He cupped her chin and raised her face to his. "Mina. I don't want to hurt you. I need to keep you safe."

Need. Not want.

"But why?"

"You know why."

She wanted so badly to ask about his scars and to ask why he cared so much about hers when he marked others. But she didn't. The only thing that mattered was keeping him in a frame of mind to want to continue protecting her.

Brian cradled her in his arms then guided her hand between his legs to return the favor he'd granted to her only moments before. She wrapped her hand around his cock and stroked over the smooth flesh. He was large, and it struck her what a waste it was that she couldn't get off from regular sex.

He ran his fingertips through her hair as she stroked him.

"Harder. I won't break."

She gripped harder, feeling like a virgin just presented with her first piece of male anatomy. He rewarded her with a sharp hiss when he came minutes later.

"Lick it up."

His voice reverberated through her, causing her stomach to tighten as she licked his skin clean.

"Good girl."

Good girl. Not *dumb whore* or *worthless slut*. Good girl. He pulled her against him. Sleep came like a wave, covering them both and pulling them down into the depths of dreams.

Eight

Brian woke before Mina. She slept soundly, snuggled into him, her small hand resting on his chest. One of her legs was slung over his. Even if at no other time, in sleep, she trusted him.

Buying her had been the heat of the moment—instinct. The week leading up to taking possession of her, he'd shoved all petty details to the back of his mind. He'd been afraid to hope things would go according to plan. Until the transfer cleared the bank and the collar was made and locked around her throat and the formal ceremony was over, he couldn't let himself trust it.

It was only now that he was able to breathe, to think, to realize what he'd acquired. He'd never intended to buy his own slave. Why would he want to? Why would he need to? He could do whatever he wanted with the women already here at the house. He didn't want the attachment. He didn't have the self-control not to damage anyone who was with him too long.

Protecting Mina was his highest priority, but what would happen if the dark thing inside him demanded her blood? Brian barely restrained it with others.

How would he control it with someone he'd developed this obsession toward?

He heard Lindsay's voice in his mind, chiding him, giving him psychological platitudes, analyzing him, explaining, no . . . concocting a *just so* story about why Brian was the way he was. It sounded good on paper when the doctor spun one of his yarns. But in the end it was only a narrative to hold the pieces in place. How could anyone ever truly know why Brian had turned the way he had?

Plenty of people were abused by monsters but didn't grow into one themselves. If Brian had turned out this way without his history, what story would Lindsay have created to explain it? Would it be an organic brain deformity? Some chemical imbalance? Or would they dig and dig until they found something troubling enough in his past to blame?

Brian slipped out from under Mina's hand and leg and rolled her onto her back. Amazingly, she slept on. This girl probably slept through hurricanes.

He pulled the sheets back and just looked at her. She was exquisite, and it angered him that someone had ever thought to lay marks across her flesh that wouldn't fade. It was a stupid thought. If the marks weren't there, Brian was sure he'd have put them there himself. He wouldn't have been able to stand to watch her waltz around upstairs perfect and unmarred. Something would have driven him to it. It was pointless to be angry over the only thing that protected her from him.

He ran his fingertips lightly over her pubic bone. Her legs fell open as if on reflex, but she didn't wake. She didn't have a full bush, but the garden had not been maintained as he liked it. From now on, she would come to him waxed.

How would he punish her? He'd committed to the idea of not physically punishing her, but nonphysical punishments might cause her to grow too comfortable, to feel she could do whatever she wanted. He hadn't bought her for the same reasons others might have, but now that he had her, he was beginning to want everything a master took from his slave.

He showered quickly and dressed. She was still asleep when he returned. He wondered if she were like sleeping beauty. Did she have to be wakened with a kiss? Would she otherwise continue to slumber despite what went on around her?

Brian took Mina's hands in turn, locking them into the shackles over the bed. It might hurt in a few hours, but the angle wasn't harsh.

She slept on.

He crossed his arms over his chest and studied her until an idea formed. Inside the nightstand drawer were several tubes: lubricants, a cream that burned—meant for punishments—and arousal cream.

Brian took the arousal cream and popped the seal. If this didn't wake her, nothing would.

He carefully opened the chest in the far corner and retrieved a spreader bar. He locked one end around each ankle. When he was satisfied she couldn't escape, he rubbed arousal cream into her clit, lingering more than was necessary, his fingers caressing the delicate folds of skin until at least that part of her awakened to his touch.

Brian pulled himself away before the rest of her could follow. But he wasn't abandoning her. He wanted to be an unseen voyeur.

The conference room on the main floor was rarely in use during the day. It had an intercom on a far wall that was more private than most of the others.

When he reached the intercom, he pressed the touch pad to gain access to his room downstairs. While any authorized person could put in a general code and use the call box to talk to people at other parts of the house, it took a more specific code to be able to listen. Brian had the only code to his room, and he'd never used it. Why would he? Unlike most of the other partners and trainers, he never kept anyone in his room.

He punched in his code. The scanner not only took in the numbers and letters he typed, but scanned his finger-print to ensure it was him. The others hadn't taken advantage of the biometric security, but privacy was vital. If they hadn't allowed for it, Brian would have vetoed an intercom in his room at all. He was too afraid someone might find his code and listen and overhear him in the middle of a nightmare.

The corners of his lips turned up as he listened to his struggling captive. Brian input another code to bring up the accompanying video feed. She thrashed on the bed, desperately seeking anything to make contact between her legs. Her pathetic mewling already made him hard. He ignored the part of his mind that warned this could be bad. He might be already unlocking a door with her that he didn't want to take her through.

He pushed the button to speak. "Mina."

Her head jerked in the direction of the call box.

"You are quite a sound sleeper. If you didn't sleep so deeply, perhaps you wouldn't be in the predicament you find yourself in now. I have some things to attend to, but I'll come downstairs to relieve you of your discomfort soon. Can you feel the metal tab attached to the shackle around your wrist?"

It reached the center of her palm and had a button. He was surprised she hadn't pressed it yet. No doubt she feared it would create an even worse outcome for her.

"Y-yes, Master."

"That's a distress button. If you push it I will come to you. But if you push it, you had better be on fire. Do we understand each other?"

"Yes, Master."

He wondered if she'd have the strength not to push it. The effects of the cream would wear off within the hour, but he planned to be back before then to hear her beg. He disconnected and went to get breakfast.

Lindsay was in the cafeteria. "Where's Mina?"

Brian glanced at his watch. "It's nine in the morning. Shouldn't you be in the city with a patient?"

"Nine o'clock Monday morning was Mina's slot. And my ten-thirty canceled. I don't have to be in the city until after lunch."

"How nice for you." Brian got in the breakfast line. The girls scrunched together to stay out of his way. He'd be lying if he said he didn't love how they cowered from him.

Lindsay wouldn't be so easily deterred. "Brian, where is she?"

"Stay out of our affairs, or I will consider you a liability."

"Are you threatening me?"

"I don't threaten. Before you trained me to be a weapon inside and outside the house, you should have paused to consider all the ways that could go wrong."

Had Lindsay believed Brian was an attack dog on a leash? That he would always obey his masters in gratitude for having a home and meals? As if Brian couldn't survive just fine on his own. They needed him, not the other way around.

Before Lindsay could bluster and protest, Brian took a cell phone from his pocket and dialed a number inside the house. The girl on the other end answered on the third ring.

"Shannon? I'm sending a girl up to you for waxing. You know how I like them."

"B-Brian. I-I mean S-sir," she stammered. He hadn't had cause to speak to Shannon directly in a while. And he knew she avoided encountering him.

"Don't worry. My business with you is done. You aren't on my radar anymore." He heard the stifled crying on the other end of the line and smirked. "What time can you see my girl?"

"E-eleven-thirty."

"Good. Make a standing appointment, and let her know the waxing schedule when she arrives. I get so irritated if my specifications aren't met, you know. I don't want to be put in a position to be irritated."

"Y-yes, Sir."

He disconnected the call and took the tray from the woman behind the counter. "Thanks, Phyllis." He turned to find Lindsay in his path. "Are you still here?"

"Brian, I sold her to you because you promised . . ."

"Right. And trusting the promises of a sociopath is a brilliant way to run your life, isn't it?" It had been a long time since Brian had been in the position to cause the doctor visible distress. He relished it.

"Brian, please. Don't hurt her. Remember, she's like you."

Brian had no intention of harming Mina; he simply enjoyed upsetting Lindsay. It was rare to be able to make him afraid. Why shouldn't Brian take every opportunity to goad the bastard? Especially when he knew any threat the doctor could devise would be hollow at best.

"Don't tell me who she is!" Brian snarled. "Get the fuck away from me!"

Lindsay backed off, then left the cafeteria. He didn't move as fast as others nearby had, but at least he went away.

Mina squeezed her eyes tight and breathed, as if breathing would make it go away. She'd woken to a sharp tingling between her legs. At first she'd thought Brian was touching her, but she quickly realized that wasn't the case. She squirmed and twisted, trying to find a way to satisfy the intense arousal. It went beyond an urge. It went beyond need.

She'd been so distracted she hadn't noticed the button nestled in her palm—not until Brian came on the intercom and explained it to her.

Last night she'd started to feel what? Attracted to him? She wasn't sure. He'd been so . . . kind. The attraction hadn't diminished this morning. But what he was doing now . . . it wasn't that it was terribly wrong, but there was a sadism in it. What if he pushed and pushed and over time hurt her?

As foolish as it was, she was beginning to believe he didn't *want* to hurt her, but if he was playing mildly sadistic games on day two . . . what would happen on month two or year two?

The door opened and Brian stepped in with a tray. He placed it on a side table. "I'm sorry I didn't get you anything hot this morning. Just a pastry and fruit. I didn't want to get you something that wouldn't taste right cold."

"Please . . ." She struggled against the chains.

He sat beside her and began stroking her hair and the side of her face. The gesture would be sweet and appreciated if there weren't other places she needed to be stroked. And Brian knew it. He didn't know how to be anything other than a sadist.

He unlocked her hands, but left her feet in the spreader bar. She hadn't noticed the pain in her arms. She'd been too focused on the one thing she needed to happen to make the world right again.

But now that her hands were released, she didn't dare make a move, no matter how much the aroused flesh between her legs demanded to be touched.

"I'm impressed. You certainly don't lack training, despite what the good doctor implied. That pleases me very much."

A blush crept up her neck. It was a horrible moment to have an attack of shyness. She wanted to cover herself and was thankful for the patch of hair that covered her like a fig leaf from a piece of biblical art. One less layer of exposure to cope with.

He sat beside her. "Do your arms hurt?"

"Yes, Master."

He took one arm and then the other and massaged the soreness out of them. He was almost as good as Anton—which was unexpected, since Anton was a professional, and Brian's only known skill set was causing pain.

She desperately needed to come, and instead he was massaging the soreness out of her arms. He arranged her hands as if she were a life-sized doll, placing them on either side of her mound, mere centimeters from the aching need.

"You'd better not so much as twitch toward touching yourself."

It took every ounce of concentration and willpower not to flick her thumb over her clit, but Brian's hard stare and the anxiety that look created within her, helped her manage the needed self-control.

"Still impressed," he said.

He picked her up and slung her over his shoulder as if he were a fireman rescuing her from a burning building. Mina tensed as he carried her from the room. She was too afraid to ask where he was taking her. Surely not upstairs. All she could think about was Jason passing her around. Would Brian do that? Why wouldn't he? She hadn't even thought to list *no sharing* on her limits— which was insane, given how much it upset her when Jason had done it.

Brian pushed one of the dungeon cell doors open and carried her in.

"N-no, please. Please. You promised. Please don't hurt me, Master."

"Shhhh. I'm not hurting you."

But what he did next didn't reinforce hope. Brian draped her over a spanking horse, so that her legs straddled it. They were still trapped immobile by the spreader bar he had yet to unlock. Even if he didn't bind her in any other way, she couldn't run or crawl away.

She whimpered, and the tears she'd fought to hold back came spilling forth. His hand was gentle on her back as he caressed her skin.

"Do you still want to come?"

She was afraid to answer. She didn't know what the right answer was. Which one would get her beaten? Which one would set her free? She didn't want anything right now as much as she wanted safety. Even the insistent throbbing between her legs took a back seat to her self-preservation instinct.

"Tell me. Now. The truth."

"Y-yes, Master."

He pressed a button on the side of the spanking horse, and it came to life, vibrating underneath her.

"Grind into it like a good girl."

He didn't have to tell her twice. The dual relief of stimulation between her legs and him not hitting her was enough to send her over the edge after only a few seconds. But he kept her there and made her come several times before he turned the vibrator off. The vinyl padding felt slippery underneath her, and she flushed, embarrassed by how wet she'd made it.

Brian didn't comment. He unshackled her feet and went to sit in a chair at the other end of the room he used to torture the poor women unfortunate enough to catch his eye or be sent to him.

He unbuttoned his pants. "I want your warm mouth wrapped around my cock."

Mina slid off the spanking horse and crawled across the floor. How could any of this be okay? How was it possible that she wanted to do this with him, after the others? There was a loneliness inside of him that reached out to the loneliness inside of her.

As she kissed and licked and sucked him, his fingers threaded through her hair—comforting her. How could this be the man she'd been afraid of? All she wanted was to please him.

"That's it. Such a good little cocksucker."

She froze. Jason's friends had made the same comment. She had to forcibly remind herself that she wasn't being passed around down here. It was only Brian. And he didn't know the history of those words.

He stopped her. "Look at me."

She looked up, surprised to find concern in his eyes.

"Are you all right? You left me for a second."

She hadn't thought it possible for a man to be more perceptive than Lindsay with the fancy degrees lining his walls and books to decipher the inner workings of the mind and human behavior. But Brian saw each shift in her demeanor. He saw things she didn't realize she was broadcasting.

"I'm fine, Master." She went back to servicing him, but his hand on her shoulder stopped her.

"Mina, I've warned you about lying to me. Do. Not. Lie."

She cringed and shrank from his tone. It took so little to erase trust.

"I asked if you were all right."

She shook her head, her gaze trained on the floor. She couldn't look at him.

"Come here." He pulled her onto his lap and cradled her in his arms.

She could barely let herself breathe, afraid even the tiniest movement might shatter whatever this was forming between them. Jason and the others had play acted at being kind at first, but they never increased in kindness or concern. Could Brian really care?

Oh, she didn't think he loved her. They barely knew each other. She didn't think they'd have some great romance like in books and movies. But did he care, as one human to another about her pain? It seemed utterly impossible that he had the capacity, given the pain he seemed to so gleefully deliver to others.

"Tell me," he said.

She wanted to play dumb, to pretend she didn't know what he wanted her to confess, but she was too afraid of breaking this new intimacy. She'd seen a hint of it the night before when their hands had touched in the shower —and she wanted more. She was starved for it.

"My last master—"

"You've never had a real master. You had an abusive asshole that played games with you that were to his advantage and not yours."

True. And now she had a *real* master in the sense of someone who wasn't playing a game with her, and everyone in the house knew how much he liked hurting people.

"Continue."

"Jason," she corrected. "He used to share me with his friends, and they'd all go on about what a good little cocksucker I was."

"Sharing upsets you."

"Yes."

"But you know I can't be exclusive. I'm going to be with others down here. And with your list of limits, exclusivity was never in the cards with any master."

"No, I mean . . . being passed around. I-I don't care about the other." She cared that he hurt others, but she didn't care that he fucked them. Though maybe that was because it all existed as something to feed his sadism.

It was obvious that what had taken place between the two of them was a whole other zone of reality. Mina thought that if he were to be tender with someone else, it might pose a problem for her. But shouldn't she prefer him to be tender with others than to be violent with them?

He guided her hand to circle around his cock. "I'll let you do it this way for now. When you feel you've worked through this, you can come to me and please me with your mouth."

It only took a few minutes before his breathing deepened and he came. She didn't wait for an order this time. She licked it up as he petted her hair and pressed a kiss to the top of her head.

"Go shower, have breakfast, do whatever you need to do. At eleven-thirty, I want you to go to room 308 on the main floor in the east wing for a waxing appointment. Then I want you in the gym working out. You need to stay fit for me. After that, you can have the rest of the day for yourself."

Mina went back to their room, but Brian didn't follow. She used the bathroom and washed her face and got in the shower. For the first time she noticed the thickness and strength of the shower glass. It could bear weight. The proof was the shackles built into the shower wall.

The spa was tucked away in a far corner of the east wing, nearly deserted.

"Hey!"

Mina turned to find Annette getting a pedicure.

"Most of the girls don't know about this place," she said conspiratorially. "Sometimes we send them before they get sold for a bit of grooming, or as a reward for something. But most of the time it's me hogging all the spa treatments. Does Brian know you're up here? I can't believe he'd send you to be pampered."

"Waxing appointment," Mina said.

"Oh." Annette's *oh* was like an encyclopedia's worth of verbiage. They both knew what that *oh* meant. It was, *Oh, of course, a sadist would send you to get waxed.*

"Should I even ask what you're waxing?"

A girl who worked in the salon approached them. "Everything," she said. Her name tag read, *Shannon*.

Mina couldn't stop the gasp. Shannon wore a low-cut tank top. Harsh scars covered her arms and whipped around her chest, a few inching up her neck. One had gotten her cheek. "What happened to you—"

"Mina . . . don't," Annette said.

Shannon smiled, but it wasn't friendly. "Don't worry about it. She should know what she's in bed with. Brian did this to me. Once upon a time I was here to be trained and sold to someone. I was all wrapped up in the fantasy —until the day I was mildly disrespectful to your master. I didn't realize who I was speaking with, and it was only my third day in the house. He dragged me to the dungeon and he did this. It made me unsaleable. If he'd only marked my back, it might have been different, but he did too much damage in too many places. When they found out I had work experience in a spa, they decided to spare my life and keep me here."

"I-I'm sorry. I didn't know."

Shannon sneered. "Of course you didn't. He favors you, doesn't he? I could hear it in his voice when he called to make the appointment. How lucky for you to be in the favor of the house monster, protected from the one person who could ever cause you genuine harm. I wouldn't get too comfortable in that position. Wild animals don't make good house pets."

"It's not as if she picked him. Lay off her!" Annette said.

"It's okay," Mina said.

She needed to hear the truth. Brian could make her forget who he was, what he was. She could put it all in a box and never look into it. But the moment she stepped outside of that bubble, she was confronted with one more reason why she had to guard her heart against this man. She couldn't allow herself to want to be near him. She'd melted too easily into his embrace in the dungeon.

She'd allowed his kind words and gentle touch to soothe and make her forget. How did he know how to be gentle? Where could he have possibly learned such a thing? She had no evidence he'd ever carefully touched another living being in his life. And yet, when his hands were on her, they brought pleasure or comfort, not pain.

"Your room is set up," Shannon said. "Come on back when you're ready." Her eyes seemed to light at the prospect of causing Brian's slave pain—as if Mina were a proxy for her master, as if somehow it would bypass her nerve endings to reach his instead.

Mina started to follow her back but Annette's hand on her arm stopped her. "I'm sorry about Shannon. I can't believe he'd send you to her."

"I can." It was obvious he wanted to strip away all her illusions. He didn't slink in the dark doing what he did. He did it in the open, leaving the evidence spread out proudly for all to see. He hadn't hidden the girl he'd punished the other day. He hadn't cared that Mina had seen. It was as if he wanted her to see—as if he dared her to challenge him or cringe from the truth.

Annette shrugged. "The only thing he doesn't do is lie."

Small consolation. Because lies were about shame or avoiding consequences. There were no consequences for Brian in this house, and he had no shame. So what was there to be dishonest about? How could it be a virtue when it cost him nothing?

"Mina?" Annette pressed.

"Yeah?"

"If I were you, I would take whatever good I could find in him. You shouldn't have to recoil even from a gentle touch just because of who delivered it. I've never seen him be kind to anyone. If he's really being that way with you, I'd do whatever I had to do to prolong it."

Annette had read her mind.

Brian was running on the treadmill when Mina entered the gym. She wore the same gym shorts and t-shirt the other girls wore for workouts and lounging around the house. When their eyes met, she looked away quickly, and he knew it wasn't just a submissive reflex. Shannon had probably given her an earful in the spa. Good.

He stepped off the machine and intercepted her near the door. The others watched. Half the girls seemed to be waiting to witness Mina punished for something, and the other half appeared jealous he'd give attention to anyone that wasn't filled with rage.

"Come with me." He guided her to the gym's dressing room. "Clear out!" he shouted. "Now!"

The girls—all in various states of undress—scattered out into the main gym. Brian put a chair in front of the door.

"Show me."

Mina pretended confusion, but she knew what he wanted to see. He raised a brow and sat on a bench.

"Show me," he repeated.

He watched as she let the shorts and her panties fall to the floor.

"Lift the shirt."

She did, revealing a smooth curve of skin.

"Hmmm," he said, watching her squirm. "I need a better look. Sit and spread your legs wide for me."

A lovely blush crept up her neck as she stepped fully out of the shorts and sat, spreading her legs. She wanted to obey him. He saw it in her eyes. She wanted to give him everything.

"Did it hurt?"

"Yes, Master."

"I'm sorry."

Weirdly, in a way, he was. The waxing was for his personal aesthetic and the joy of running his tongue over smooth bare flesh with no obstruction to her enjoyment or his. The pain was an incidental cost, not the point of the exercise. "Did you make another appointment?"

"Yes, Master. In five weeks."

"Good. You'll get waxed regularly for me. You will never miss an appointment."

"Master?"

"Yes?" His gaze was still riveted to the space between her legs, staring at it like he'd just seen his first cunt.

"Shannon said you left those scars on her."

His eyes snapped to her face. "And?" he challenged. This was exactly the kind of bullshit he'd feared—that he might be coaxed to care what another being thought about him or his actions, that the one freedom he'd had in his life . . . the freedom of just not giving a shit, could be so easily torn from him. If it could, he was no better than the sniveling boy he once was, crying and cowering locked under the stairs. The only freedom was not giving a shit. And yet, Mina made him care about something beyond his own sadism. Fuck her for that. But even as the anger welled up, it turned his stomach again and then quieted down.

"N-nothing, Master."

"Nothing is right. You do not question me or my actions. You are not in a position to judge me or control my behavior. Quite the opposite, in fact."

She started to cry. Brian stood and closed the distance between them. He carefully ran his tongue over the tears on her cheek. He needed to taste her pain. Then he held her close.

"Mina, you didn't choose this. You didn't choose me. This isn't your fault. You are just a puppet on my stage, and when I say dance, you'll dance."

He pressed two fingers inside her and reveled in her exquisite wetness, then he knelt between her legs and licked the smooth, freshly waxed skin until he felt her succumb to him. Her fingers threaded in his hair, and she moaned.

"Louder," he said. "I want them all to hear you surrender to me."

Her whimpers and groans grew more intense until he was sure there could be no doubt what was happening in the dressing room. When she finally shuddered and came, he stood smoothly.

"Get dressed, and get on the treadmill. I want a thirty minute run out of you, then we'll hit the weights."

He left the dressing room to let her get herself together. The girls in the gym gaped at him, but as he met each of their eyes, they turned quickly away. The bitter hatred was painted starkly across their faces. He could practically hear the thoughts in their heads: *Why is Mina so special?*

He wanted to take them to his dungeon for private one-on-one sessions until they each admitted they were filthy entitled trash just like his stepmother, until they begged him to forgive them for daring to think they were worth his protection or care.

Nine

*T*he music's too loud. It was the signal things were about to go bad. It meant they were all downstairs waiting for her. Jason and his friends. Would it be less horrible if it was only him? She should have left already. But now, she was trapped at least for the night. They'd take her and tie her down. There would be no going anywhere until they'd each had their turn.

"Mina," Jason called her. "Come out come out wherever you are."

His voice drew closer. God, why hadn't she left this afternoon while he was out? And go where? And do what?

She was running out of places to hide in his house. He always found her.

The closet door opened and coats were shoved back. He dragged her out as she held on to the door frame, her fingernails digging into the wall.

"Don't be a tease." He grabbed her hand and pressed it against the front of his pants. "Don't you feel what you do to me? This is what you do to all of us. We're all hard and ready for you. We need you. You know you want to be our good little whore."

"No, no no no. Please stop. Please," she sobbed, knowing Jason wouldn't stop. He wouldn't stop talking or dragging her down the stairs to the other waiting men. He liked the tears. And the begging. It turned him on.

"Shhhh shhhhh. It's just a dream."

The arms that had felt restraining were more gentle now. Brian. He'd woken her from the dream, rescued her from Jason. But what good would that rescue be if he simply dragged her farther into a different nightmare?

Jason had taken her from herself, but now she was with a bigger monster. There was no question Brian was the bigger monster. But he was holding her and rocking her and kissing her hair, whispering "shhhhh" . . . soothing her. As if she could be soothed anymore. As if there were any pieces of her that could ever fit back together again.

It was a lie. It had to be a lie. It had to be the game they all played to make her trust before they pulled it all away. But she couldn't help melting further into his arms, sagging against him, releasing the heavy weight she carried even for just a minute until reality sharpened in front of her—the reality that Brian didn't have the capacity to save anyone. She'd seen it in his hard flat stare. He was stone in there. Why did she keep looking for someone to save her? To protect her? To dominate her in some fantasy gentle way that if it existed could never exist for her?

Brian steadied her as her breath moved back to a normal cadence and her tears began to dry. Slowly his hold on her loosened, and he untangled himself from the sheets. She tried not to look at him, tried not to want him. He'd wreck her worse than Jason. He put on sweatpants and tennis shoes. Then he dropped a t-shirt, gym shorts, and shoes on the bed for her.

"Get dressed."

"W-what? Why?"

"Why, Master."

She flinched as if he might punish her for the slip, for talking to him as if they were roommates instead of property and owner. But no retribution came.

"Why, Master?"

"I can't hit you, but you need pain."

She scrambled back, shaking her head violently. "No." She couldn't bring herself to say "you promised". What did his promise mean? She'd known it was empty from the beginning. She'd just hoped his mercy might stretch longer than this.

His voice turned soft. "That's not what I meant. I would never . . . You need catharsis. You need something physical to unwind this thing inside you that's eating you alive. I know this." He took her hands in his. And she believed he knew exactly where she'd been. He'd been in the same dark place somehow.

"You need to *run*," he said.

The word sounded much as it had in the corridor that first night. And it carried the same urgency now that it had then. It made everything inside her unfreeze. It made movement possible. It made breathing possible.

Run.

Was that why he ran so much on the treadmill? Trying to outrun his demons? Did it ever work?

When she'd dressed, Brian led her up the stairs to the main level. The house slumbered so deep it was as if a spell had been cast over it. It seemed nothing would wake the inhabitants. All that existed were Brian and Mina—him tugging her hand, pulling her insistently through the darkened house. The lights near the floor cast an eerie, ghostly glow upon everything they touched.

When they reached the gym, he only turned one set of lights on, the rest of the space stayed dark.

He set the program on the treadmill and took the machine beside her, setting the same program. "Run. Don't stop until you can't go anymore."

Mina ran. She ran to him, away from him, away from everyone and everything, away from the dreams, away from Jason, away from her brokenness and the pieces she couldn't reach to pick up.

She didn't look at him. He didn't look at her. No music played. It was just the sound of shoes hitting the moving platform over and over.

Half an hour later, she couldn't go anymore. She stopped the program and collapsed on the floor trying to catch her breath. Brian was still going strong. How much did he run? It seemed as if his life was a string of coping mechanisms for the violence that shaped him still.

Brian got off the treadmill and pulled her to her feet. "Shower next, then food."

It was a carefully orchestrated ritual. How many nights had he done this? How many nights had it been him waking from a nightmare instead of her? He was letting her into something private, and for the first time it didn't feel like a game or an act. It felt like intimacy. Understanding. If only it was real.

Showering was another silent ritual, both of them squeezed inside, his hands running carefully over her with the soap. But that was all he did.

He shut the water off, toweled off, and dressed. Mina echoed him and started to put her own clothes back on.

"No."

Her hand froze over the clothes.

"Just wrap the towel around you and come with me."

She followed him down the dark silent hallways until he stopped at a door at the end of one hall. He punched in a code and pushed the door open.

She hesitated. It was the medical room. She felt the panic wrap around her throat as the memories of the last time she was here flooded back. She'd been spared that time.

"Go on," Brian said, nudging her.

She stepped inside as he locked the door behind them and flicked on the lights.

He crossed to the bigger spotlights and turned them on. They sputtered to life as they slowly woke and brightened the room further. He set up the video camera and positioned it near the medical equipment, lining up what he wanted to film.

"Drop the towel," he said.

"M-Master . . ."

He stepped out from behind the camera. "No one else will see it. It's just for me. If you don't want to do it, we can just go eat. It's okay. I'm not going to hurt you." He'd closed the distance between them. He caressed her cheek with the back of his hand. "Will you be a good girl for me and let me do the exam? After all, I never got the full clean bill of health from the doctor on you. I need to know what I bought, don't you think? All the other buyers get to see this."

His tone was light, teasing. While he'd been kind to her, having a moment of teasing from him was a new side entirely. It made her want to do it.

"Drop the towel."

Mina's hand unclenched, and the terrycloth fluttered to the floor.

He bent his head, and his tongue flicked across first one nipple, then the other. They hardened when the cool air hit.

"Good. I want, hard pert little nipples in my film. Will you do this for me, Mina?"

"Yes, Master."

"Good girl. Get on the table. Feet in the stirrups. I'm sure you've been to the doctor before. You know how this goes."

She climbed onto the table and did as he asked while he put on a white lab coat and blue surgical gloves. He snapped the gloves on. The red light on the camera blinked as it hovered over the examining table with a clear unobstructed view of her.

He picked up a clipboard with some papers on it and made a show of studying it, even though she knew he was just making a cheesy porno with her. The only thing missing was the bad music.

"Hmmmm Ms. Calloway, when was your last visit?" He looked up, clearly expecting her to go along with it.

For the smallest space of time, she felt something softer for him beginning to form. It was a terrible idea to let that seed take root, but he was playing a game with her. A lighthearted sexual game—the kind of thing she'd wanted before but had never been given. How could he be so brutal to others and do this with her?

"Ms. Calloway? It's important that you are very honest with me about your medical history. Or else how can I *treat* you?"

"Uh . . . about a year," she said.

"And how many partners have you had? I mean, I'm your doctor. Surely the exact details of your sex life are my business. I'm only trying to help you."

He made it sound as smug and paternalistic as possible. A laugh escaped her.

Brian sat on a rolling stool and moved closer, his hands on her knees, pushing the stirrups wider apart. His intense gaze met hers, but it was tempered with amusement. "Is something funny?"

"N-no, Doctor. Nothing's funny. Fifty partners since my last check-up," she lied.

"Fifty!" he exclaimed. "We'll have to test you for everything. So slutty. Nurse! I need the full panel of slut tests, stat!"

Mina held back another laugh, afraid if she laughed too much he wouldn't finish this. Unbelievably, she wanted him to, now.

Before she had time to think, a cold, metal speculum was inside her. "I'm going to make you watch this video later," he whispered for her instead of the camera, "so you can get a good look at what your doctor has been looking at all these years."

The thought should have bothered her, but right now it just turned her on. After a few minutes, he removed the cold metal, then gloved fingers were inside her, exploring, feeling all her most intimate private places.

"With your prolific sexual misadventures, I think you should come in for more frequent check-ups. Don't you agree, Ms. Calloway?"

"Y-yes, Doctor."

He smirked as he withdrew his fingers. "There's one more test I need to conduct. At some point, I'm sure you'll wish to settle down with one man. Many husbands feel anxious about their wife's sexual response. So we like to test that. Just so they know it's not them."

He rolled the stool over to a drawer and pulled out a vibrator. Mina's breath caught when the buzzing started. Then he turned it off and came back to her.

"I'd first like you to manually stimulate yourself for me."

The game was becoming less funny and oddly more exciting as he intently watched her hand move between her legs.

He made a show of writing notes on the clipboard while she stroked the aroused flesh between her thighs.

"Good. Now slip your fingers inside."

Her hips bucked off the table, her feet pressing hard into the metal stirrups as her fingers pumped in and out.

"Do you feel how wet you are?"

"Y-yes, Doctor," she whimpered, barely able to maintain a coherent conversation.

"That's what the husbands and boyfriends want. They want you dripping wet and ready for them. I'm very pleased with your response."

He turned the vibrator back on and pressed it against her clit. "Hold it there and come while I examine your breasts. If you climax, keep going. It's necessary for our records."

By this point he could say any ridiculous thing in the world and she was too far gone to giggle. He put the clipboard down and stood next to her, his hands kneading her breasts in the same impersonal way as a doctor would, but then his thumbs brushed over her nipples, and he pinched one as she came, tears sliding down her cheeks from the force of her orgasm.

He moved back to the stool and took the vibrator from her. "Touch your breasts. You need to know how to do it properly."

She stroked her breasts as he kept the vibrator pressed against her, not releasing her until she'd climaxed several more times.

Finally, he turned the toy off and dropped it in a bin marked "sanitize".

Mina lay there watching him as he removed the gloves and tossed them in the trash and draped the lab coat over the counter. He turned the camera off and took out the tape. He picked up the towel, draping it over her, as if protecting her modesty.

He pressed a kiss against her forehead. "Do you feel better?"

"Yes, Master."

Mina sat in a chair beside a stainless steel island in the large kitchen behind the cafeteria. She watched while Brian retrieved milk, eggs, cheese, salt, and pepper from the fridge—then bread from the bread box. She couldn't believe this man would ever let a carb pass through his lips.

They didn't speak while he made toast and scrambled eggs. Her mind kept going back to the medical room and how in the still spaces with him, everything felt unbroken. She didn't know how it was possible for someone so fucked up to make her feel *not* fucked up. Tonight she'd gotten the first real glimpse of the man he could have been if not for the scars that had painted a different person. He was in pieces, like her. Tonight she'd seen one of the better ones.

He put a plate in front of her and sat beside her. They ate in silence. She felt calmer after the running and the shower and the game. Brian finished before she did and left the room. Had he gone back downstairs?

Jason had never taken care of her like this. He'd never held her when she was scared or made a meal for her. It had always been about him. If she dared complain, they were back to *You're not a real sub!*

So far those words hadn't left Brian's mouth.

He returned and dropped a piece of paper and a pen down next to her plate.

"Give me the names of the men who created you."

Mina looked up, the calm slipping away again. "I-I'm sorry? I-I don't know what you mean."

He leaned in, his gaze level with hers, staring her down. "You know exactly what I'm asking for. Give me their names and any additional information that will make my search shorter."

"W-what are you going to do?" Deep down she knew. Something violent. Maybe something fatal. "I-it was consensual."

It wasn't.

No matter how many times she told herself that lie. Nothing with them had been consensual except on the surface in the beginning. When she'd been sold to Brian she'd known she had no real choices, and yet when he touched her, her soul said yes to him.

"No! The response you are looking for here is: Yes. Master." He crossed his arms over his chest and watched as she wrote down the names of the men who had broken her.

She considered making up names—unsure if she could be the cause of whatever Brian would do to them—but she was afraid she might give him names of real people—innocent people who didn't deserve whatever he planned to mete out.

"I-I don't know the names of Jason's friends . . ."

"He will tell me."

Mina was sure that was true. She handed the paper to Brian.

He scanned it. "Is this all you know?"

"Y-yes, Master."

He folded the paper and put it in the pocket of his sweatpants. He put the empty plates in the sink, and they went downstairs.

Brian watched Mina undress; this time the self-consciousness had left her.

"Back in bed. You need rest," he said.

She dutifully got back in, and he pulled the blankets over her. He crossed to the CD player and put in his copy of Chopin's nocturnes. He put it on repeat just as his mother had once done with the records. As an adult, he'd listened to this disc many nights to go back to sleep. When he couldn't hurt someone, when he'd run as far as his body would let him and it still wasn't enough, the nocturnes helped. It was how he'd known they would somehow carry Mina through the withdrawal.

He'd wanted to go to her those nights, hold her, help her through it. But he was unused to putting broken things back together. He didn't know how to comfort or soothe, and he'd wanted to delay her knowledge of the monster she'd be trapped with forever. He'd wanted everything to be perfect. The music, the collar, easing her through the ceremony. So maybe she wouldn't fear him. He'd wanted to buy her trust. But there wasn't enough money in the world for such a purchase.

He couldn't begin to imagine what had come over him in the auction prep room. He'd planned to be more serious, but when he'd tested the first joke and the fear around her had melted like a block of ice exposed to sun, he just wanted to make her smile more, laugh more. He wanted to see her happy.

He changed clothes and put on sturdy boots. She watched him silently from the bed. She wouldn't ask where he was going. She knew better than to ask.

"Sleep," he said. "Everything will be okay."

But would it? Could it ever be okay? Had it become okay for him?

She hesitated, then closed her eyes. He touched her face, and she leaned into him, her features relaxing. He slipped quietly out of the room and closed the door.

Brian kept a bag in his SUV for occasions like this. The last time had been official business. He'd been sent by Lindsay to stop someone from talking. But this was personal. Almost as personal as his stepmother had been.

He stopped by Lindsay's office to use the computer to search the names on the list along with the scant details Mina had jotted down that might give Brian a starting point. The internet search filled in the blanks within minutes. He made some notes to add to Mina's and cleared the search history.

The sun was barely peaking over the horizon when he reached the first name on the list. Jason.

It would be just about time for him to be going off to work if he worked normal hours doing normal things.

The neighborhood was mostly empty—a lot of houses for sale in a new housing development. No witnesses. Perfect. He should have planned things out, and he would after the first one. He just needed to get one of them done. Mina hadn't realized it, but she'd dug the pen into the paper deeper on this name. This was the one that caused the dreams—that strangled scream she'd made that had woken him from a dead sleep, the sweating, the panic. He knew that scream, that panic.

Maybe he should wait, let Jason be last. But Brian wanted to take this one at the height of his rage. He needed catharsis. Something physical. Something that hurt . . . someone else.

He grabbed his bag out of the back seat, took one final look around the neighborhood to ensure it was truly deserted, then made his way to the front door.

Birds called each other, but stopped as he approached. A dog barked in the distance. It was unseasonably warm and sunny today, a brief pause on winter before it snapped back into bright bitter cold again. It was the perfect day to do this. An unassuming happy day for Mina's biggest tormentor.

Brian set the bag on the ground and knocked. No answer. He rang the bell. Still no answer. He pressed his finger on the button again, holding it down until the door was ripped open.

"What!" a man on the other end barked.

"Hello. I'm Brian Sloan. I'm here on behalf of Mina Calloway."

The man laughed and shook his head. "Cute. You must be the heroic new boyfriend."

"No. This is a different story."

"Yeah, okay, hero. Did she cry to you about how mean I was to her? She consented to all of it. Little whore tops from the bottom. But you probably know that by now. Tell that cunt when I told her to get out, I didn't mean send her newest fuck to beat me up."

Keep talking, asshole.

Jason started to shut the door in his face, but Brian's boot stopped it from closing.

"I'm happy to say I'm not here to beat you up." He picked up the bag and forced his way inside, slamming and locking the door behind him.

Outside, the birds resumed their conversation.

Mina had just made it to the top of the stairs when she heard shouting in the main entry hall.

"What the fuck is all this?" Lindsay shouted.

She moved down the hallway and peered around the corner into the entryway. Brian stood surrounded by several bags he'd hauled inside. He was covered in blood.

"It's trash," Brian replied coolly.

"Who?" Lindsay said. "We agreed we'd manage this and that you wouldn't just go off . . ."

"We agreed to nothing. I said it's trash. It needs to be burned. If you'll excuse me."

"Brian . . ."

He rounded on the doctor. "You use me. You've always used me. Do you think I don't know that? You used me. You used Mina. It's all about you getting what you want, what helps your bank account. I'm not the fucking idiot you seem to think I am!"

Mina rushed down the hall and back down the stairs to the room at the end of the corridor. She should have closed the door and stayed hidden inside with the Chopin still playing on repeat. But she watched through the crack as Brian brought the bags down and took them to the hidden door behind the stairs.

When he emerged again, he was naked—his clothes and shoes likely burning with the rest of the evidence. The look in his eyes was like nothing she'd ever seen. Nothing she wanted to ever see again.

She backed up when he opened their door. He looked wild. Savage. As if he'd ripped some animal apart with his bare hands and teeth. No. As if he were the animal.

"I need to get cleaned up."

The CD ended and went back to the first nocturne.

"Who?" she said, echoing Lindsay's question upstairs.

"Jason. The rest will be taken care of. Don't worry."

Her breath hitched. Jason was gone. Like God just erased his mistake.

She didn't know what to feel. She didn't know what she was supposed to feel. Yes, Jason had abused her, but she'd consented to . . . she'd agreed to . . . It wasn't as if he'd kidnapped her or held her against her will. She'd chosen . . . and now . . .

The bathroom door shut and the shower came on.

What was she giving her heart to?

Ten

Brian didn't need to kill. He was largely indifferent to the act, but he would do it when he felt he needed to.

For the past three weeks, Brian had moved down Mina's list, eliminating a few unnecessary genes from the evolutionary pool every few days until it was taken care of. Some of them had lived in different states. That helped. And he never killed the same way twice. Killing the same way twice was stupid. No sense in hitting law enforcement radars. They were drawn to big body counts like flies to corpses.

Three weeks. It seemed an impossible length of time to keep his attention on a woman without hurting her. Not only had he not hurt her, he hadn't fucked her, either. And although she hadn't yet attempted another blow job, he hadn't pushed her.

Each time she trusted him more, he wanted to put a bigger wall around his heart. He feared what this new vulnerability could mean for him, the power she could hold over him because he cared for her. He couldn't stand this free fall with nothing to hold onto, no steady solid ground on which to stand. He hadn't been this vulnerable since he was a child. The moment he'd gotten big enough and strong enough to fight back, he'd sworn he'd never allow himself to experience a moment of vulnerability or weakness with another soul. No one would ever have the chance to gain the upper hand again. No one would ever get the drop on him.

And yet he'd allowed another person to sleep in his bed, unchained, with full knowledge that during his vulnerable hours of sleep, if she wanted to, she could find a way to end him.

But Mina let him sleep at night. Her warm body wrapped around his kept the nightmares away. Except for that first night, he hadn't had a bad dream from his past in the entire time he'd had her. And since he'd started disposing of the men who'd hurt her, she hadn't either. He was unwilling to mess with what worked.

He stepped out of the bathroom to find Mina lounging on the bed, a sheet draped over what he could tell was a nude body. She didn't speak, but she beckoned him to her with an uncertain gesture. He let the towel drop and joined her. He couldn't bring himself to speak either.

She slid down his body, kissing a trail from his neck, down his chest, over his abs, and to his cock. Her hot tongue began to lav the bundle of nerves there. Brian gripped the edge of the mattress with one hand, and petted her hair with the other. He couldn't stop touching her to make sure she was real, to reassure her she was safe with him.

Brian stayed very still as she took him fully into her mouth. He inhaled sharply as took him in deeper and sucked.

He didn't make demands or orders, afraid to break the bravery she'd found. He could barely focus on the physical pleasure, instead consumed with the fact that she'd come to him on her own, that she must have worked up to this to push all the images of other sadistic men before him out of her head. Their taunts. Their cruelty. All the things Brian unapologetically was—with everyone he'd ever touched but her.

He refused to break the spell or give her another flashback. He let out a hiss when he came and stroked her throat as it worked to swallow his release.

When he was spent, he pulled her to him so that her head rested on his chest. He ran his fingertips over the scars on her back, pausing over each one as if his fingers pressing against them enough times could erase them. He wanted to make them go away. He wanted to make her history go away.

"Y-you can fuck me if you want to. I-I mean, I know you need to recover, but . . . then after that . . . if . . . if you want," she said.

"No."

"Why? Do you not want me?"

"Not like that."

Brian continued trailing his fingertips over her skin while he tried to figure out how to express the thoughts in his head. "I don't want to fuck you, Mina. Fucking is not a compliment. Maybe others can do it and call it making love, but for me it's an act of aggression. I'm afraid if I dominate you in that way that nothing will hold me back from the other ways I could hurt you. I can't separate it from how I am with other women down here. I can't go there with you. I didn't think you wanted me to."

She released a sigh. He was sure it wasn't meant to be heard or discerned by him, but it was relief. What could have gotten into her head to make her think that the contract had changed? Or that he wanted it to?

"I thought maybe you were getting bored with me, or maybe it made you angry . . . the limits in the contract . . . and that you would just . . . take it."

Oh. She wanted to feel like she had some control.

The contract held no power over him. There was no one to enforce it. Brian was the only enforcer at the house. He had no one to answer to. It was just a piece of paper with words that he could choose to follow or not. The only reason he chose to follow them was because he couldn't be his own tormentor. And whatever evil crawled beneath his skin demanding satisfaction, passed over her when it saw her as if sacrifices had already bled to spare her his wrath.

The intercom came on, breaking the moment.

"We're sending someone down to you," Lindsay said over the speaker. "She's new and too rebellious. She's causing chaos up here with her demands. Where do you want her?"

"Put her in cell A. I'll deal with her in a few minutes."

Mina tensed beneath him. He knew she hated what he was. He wished that just being with her could soften his edges and make him good—for her. He wished he wasn't so broken and damaged. If she could understand what a miracle it was that he could be gentle with her— just one person in the entire world—maybe she would accept what he had to do. What he *wanted* to do and could muster no guilt for.

She should count herself lucky that she didn't ping his radar as someone it would be fun to harm.

He eased out of the bed. "Go upstairs for a while."

He'd been open with her. She had to accept it. Period. And yet, lately he found himself trying to shield her, to hide it. Each time, he grew more irrationally angry. As if it were her fault he was turning so soft. She was making him a liar.

"Yes, Master."

There were tears in her voice, and it enraged him. He gripped her tighter, and she gasped before he realized he'd done it.

"Go now before I say or do something I'll regret."

She looked on him with that fear again, the same fear from the first day after he'd bought her. The same fear from the night she'd met him. It would never go away. She would never trust him because he couldn't trust himself. The shared intimacy of only moments before seemed like a dream. Every time they inched toward something good, it shattered again when reality came crashing back.

Mina moved quickly down the dungeon corridor, but not quickly enough. The new girl was already being brought downstairs by Gabe. She struggled in his arms and cursed at him. She was too defiant. Brian would love breaking her.

Don't look at her. Don't think about her. Just go upstairs. It's not happening. It's not real.

If she could only narrow everything down to the small world in which she and Brian inhabited, everything would be fine. She darted past the girl and up the stairs, forcing herself not to look back.

She wished she could go to the spa with Annette and get a massage or a manicure, but Shannon had looked on her with too much accusation. Everywhere Mina turned, evidence of Brian's brutality stared her in the face. The women in the house were all waiting for her to fall, for

Brian to lose it, for her to be reduced to the same status with him that the rest of them lived in.

Besides her, only Annette was protected. And that was because she belonged to Anton. The collar protected Anton's slave in the same way Mina's collar protected her. Her fingers strayed to touch the metal at her throat.

Mina felt herself pulled back toward the dungeon. She didn't want to go down there. She didn't want to see or hear what Brian was doing. She wanted to stay upstairs where it was safe, where she could pretend that he didn't do these things.

Brian had been nothing but protective toward her. Even when he seemed angry or scary or intense, he always found another outlet. Never her. But it was in him —deeper and darker than it had been with Jason or any of the others.

He was a bomb that could go off at any moment. Any time Mina got too close, she heard the ticking. She crept down the stairs, knowing she'd regret it. But the darkness inside Brian pulled her like wispy black smoke, embracing her and calling her to him. It demanded that she watch, that she couldn't hide from what he was.

She was barely down the stairs when she heard the new girl's screams and begging. Mina had been sure the second the blindfold had come off on the day Brian bought her, that the rest of *her* life would be nothing but screaming and begging and cringing and cowering in corners. And more scars. So far she'd been shown mercy.

But the rooms underground smelled like pain and fear. And she couldn't quite convince herself that it was any better when she was spared and it was someone else taking the beatings.

Mina flinched as the whip cracked. Sometimes he was more methodical. He took his time. He mentally tortured them and worked them into a state to burn off the worst of whatever was inside him that needed sated. She knew why. If he went full out from the beginning, he might make too many of them unsaleable like Shannon in the spa. He had to ease his way in.

But today, he'd moved straight to the whip. Mina edged closer and peered through the window to find the new girl tied with her hands over her head against the pole in the center of the room.

"Please, please I swear I'll be good," she screamed. And she meant it. It had taken only a few minutes with Brian for her to realize the folly of whatever stupid thing she'd done.

"Will you?" Brian asked. "Because from what I heard you were making all sorts of demands as if you were queen of the castle. Tell me, sweetheart, do you think you're the queen, now? We had one of those once. It didn't end well for her."

"N-no, Sir!"

Crack.

"What are you, then?"

"J-just a slave."

He laughed. "Oh, you're not even fit for that yet. Right now you're just a dumb whore that might amuse me enough to let you live to be trained and sold. Do you know how many people I've killed?"

She shook her head vigorously.

"A. Lot. And I don't feel a thing except relief when another life slips away. If I spare you today, think about that when you're upstairs with one of the others—one of the gentle souls who can barely stand to venture down here because they aren't dark or hard enough for it."

"Y-yes, Sir."

The whip cracked against her skin again, and a few drops of blood hit the floor.

"I can fuck you or I can beat you some more. Which would you prefer?"

"F-fuck. Please fuck."

He laughed. "Good girl. Your smart mouth has no purpose here except to worship my cock. Do you understand?"

"Y-yes, Sir."

"The only thing I want you to think about in this house is how you can please the men who wander these halls. When you're up there being a dirty slut and you think you're being as slutty as you can possibly be, remember you can always be better. Always strive for more. You'd better if you want to stay out of the dungeon. Obey them fast. Get sold quickly. And move far from my reach."

He thrust into her, and she whimpered in something like relief. That was when he looked up to find Mina watching him. He was not happy.

She fled up the stairs. When she reached the top, she scanned the main hall, then ran outside and to the cafeteria. There was a game room in the west wing and the spa in the east. She bumped into Lindsay while trying to decide which direction to go in next.

"Where's Annette?"

He gripped her shoulders, a look of concern in his eyes. "Mina, are you all right?"

"No. I'm not all right. I will never be all right. Where is Annette? I have to talk to her!"

Anton's slave was the only person in the house that Mina felt she could be open with.

"She's meeting with some guests. She's not here right now."

Mina began to pace, not caring that she looked completely insane. The other girls in the cafeteria backed away, but managed to stay close enough to eavesdrop because apparently she was the best gossip here. Her and this sick thing with Brian.

"What happened?" Lindsay asked.

"I can't talk to you! I'm not allowed to talk to you!" She was screaming now, her voice carrying all the way out to the pool from where a few girls and trainers straggled in to watch the show unraveling before them.

"Come to my office. You need to talk. You're falling apart."

Tears streamed down her face. "I feel something for him. I don't know what but something. I can't . . . not when he . . . how can I feel anything for him when he's such a monster? How can I do anything but cringe when he touches me? What's *wrong* with me? I can't do this anymore. I can't. I can't. Why did you do this to me? Why couldn't you just follow what you said you'd do and sell me to someone kind?"

Brian groaned as he came, the new girl trembling in his arms. Her fear was intoxicating. Just the knowledge that he was in control, that he could do anything, gave him a rush like no other. He might feel peace in Mina's arms, but he felt powerful here.

He untied her, and she slid to the ground. "Go," he said, "before I decide I'm not finished with you."

She scrambled to get back into her clothing and out of the cell. He doubted he'd see her again for the rest of her stay—if she had any sense in her head at all.

Now what to do with Mina? He'd told her to go upstairs. She knew why. And yet she'd defied him. She'd slunk back down in the shadows—his little voyeur who just couldn't help touching the darkness. He'd have to do something to stop these displays of disobedience. So far it had been minor things, but he refused to let her under-mine him, to become some insufferable brat.

When he reached the top of the stairs he heard Mina yelling. He ran to the cafeteria, thinking she was being hurt, only to find her talking to Lindsay. About him. About them.

"Mina!" Brian roared. "What did I tell you? And yet you go behind my back and defy me? Me! I told you to stay the fuck away from the doctor!"

He wouldn't be affected by the terror that crossed her face. He couldn't. He couldn't let himself love her. She made him weak. This weak, helpless feeling in the center of his chest. It was worse than what he remembered. He had to stop caring. He had to stop.

He felt the walls as they grew around him to protect him from her.

Mina dropped to her knees. "Please, Master. I'm sorry. Please don't hurt me. Please."

She cringed as he got near.

Lindsay stepped in front of her. "Brian, you need to calm down. She's not betraying you. She's not doing anything wrong. She's struggling."

"I will show her struggle," he said. He gripped Lind-say around the throat and shoved him. The doctor crashed into one of the tables, upending it and sending chairs scattering on the hard floor. "Stay out of it! How many times do I have to fucking tell you? How little do you value your life?"

Mina trembled. He raised his hand, then dropped it by his side. He was so close, so close to shifting her the barest bit out of the protection box and into a box he could deal with. Something familiar. Something that would release the knots tied inside of him instead of tie them tighter. But all he could see was the marks on her back and the stairs and the darkness and the twisted rage of his stepmother's face as she raised the switch over and over. All he could hear was that stupid dog whimpering and then him whimpering and Mina whimpering. Only her whimpering was real—happening now.

The people who'd been crowded around when he reached the cafeteria, backed away quietly, as if trying to make themselves invisible from him. Good instincts.

Brian stalked across the room and grabbed the first girl he came to.

"NO!" she screamed, trying to struggle from his grasp, but he held firm.

Mina looked up, confused.

"Are you familiar with the concept of whipping boys, Mina?"

She shook her head. "I-I mean yes. I know what they are. W-what they were. D-don't do this. Please, Master. Take me. Please."

He laughed. "Such bravery all of a sudden. What happened to begging me not to hurt you? I'm sorry, but you will not defy me. If you persist in your disobedience, I will be forced to punish someone in your place." He started to drag the girl from the room and looked back to find Mina struggling to her feet, a look of indecision on her face.

"Mina, come with me," Brian said. "This, you will not be shielded from."

He didn't look back to see if she was following. He knew she was following. He took the girl to an empty cell he hadn't used in a while and shoved her into a chair and strapped her down. Mina hovered behind him in the doorway.

"Please take me. Please don't do this," she whispered. "She hasn't done anything wrong."

He stormed across the floor to her, and she cringed. "Is that an admission of your own guilt? First you sneak back down here and watch through the window while I'm punishing someone after I told you to go upstairs. Then you go to Lindsay and share our private business."

"Master, I'm sorry. Please. Please just let her go."

"No!" He grabbed Mina's wrist and dragged her to a second chair and strapped her down. "I am going to punish her, and you are going to watch. Since you can't seem to stop yourself from watching. Here, have a front row seat. Enjoy the show. Let me entertain you."

He couldn't stop the words flying out of his mouth. He couldn't feel anything. Everything shut down. Her wrist was red from where he'd grabbed her so hard.

A dead weight settled in his stomach, a looming dread, seeing how easily he could hurt her. What was she doing to him? Why was this happening? He wanted it to be simple. He wanted to keep everything in compartments so he could go on. She was trying to break him apart. What would happen if he just punished her? How guilty would he feel? How much would it hurt him? Maybe he could push through it and retain what he needed to protect himself from . . . from whatever.

He left the room and slammed the door. He paced the dungeon corridor taking steady deep breaths, trying to think. He couldn't think straight. The rage consumed him. How had he gotten here? This war between protecting her and possessing her?

After several minutes he gained enough control to go back inside. He shut the door calmly and locked it and made his way to the two bound women. Both seemed ready to come out of their skin with fear.

"Mina, you shouldn't be afraid. I'm not going to hurt you." He turned to the other girl. "This one on the other hand . . ."

The other girl whimpered and struggled and shot death glares at Mina.

"You're a monster," Mina said.

"Yes, but you knew that the moment you laid eyes on me. And you still crave me. You want my hands on you. You seek my comfort. You move closer to me in your sleep despite what I am."

He bent to kiss her. When his mouth touched hers, she melted beneath him.

He pulled back. "That's what I thought." He nudged her knees open and slipped his fingers underneath her gym shorts and panties. He smiled in triumph at the wetness there. He'd known she would be wet for him because she was always wet for him now. It didn't matter what he was. Or what he did. She was lost.

Brian turned his attention to the other girl, and the room pulled into sharp focus. The calm settled over him again, and he began to lay out his tools.

Eleven

Mina squeezed her eyes shut. A few times, Brian had caught her doing it and made her open them, but whenever she could put distance between her and what was happening she did. Though there was no distance great enough. This girl was down here because of her.

Why hadn't Mina just listened to him? Why hadn't she remained upstairs and away while he did what he did? If she had, she wouldn't have had the meltdown. She could have waited to talk to Annette privately somewhere, instead of spilling it in front of everyone to Lindsay.

"Mina . . . if you close your eyes once more, I will start over again, and I don't think our toy can take much more."

She forced her eyes open. Brian had completely lost it. He'd cut the girl. He'd whipped her. He'd fucking *branded* her. That brand might make her unsaleable. If it did, he might end up killing her.

"Maybe I should keep her in the house to punish whenever you do something wrong. Tell me, would you like to be Mina's whipping girl?"

The girl had gone someplace else inside herself.

"I hate you," Mina said.

Brian backhanded the girl in the chair, and she reeled back. "Say it again, Mina. I'll bitch slap her every time you speak to me that way. I don't care if you hate me, but if you do, you will motherfucking keep it to yourself."

Now wasn't the time to test him or push his buttons. He seemed even more unhinged than usual. She pressed her lips into a firm line, willing herself to keep her anger and hatred for this man bottled up. How could she have thought she was developing feelings for him? And love? How could she allow that thought into her mind?

Brian didn't deserve love. He should be put down like any rabid dog. He was too broken to be anything but a danger to society. She could no longer excuse his behavior. She felt drained, exhausted, as if she'd taken the punishment herself. But to even think that way was awful because her skin remained unbroken.

"Mina, will you speak to Lindsay again?" Brian asked, his voice low and calm.

"No, Master."

"Will you come down here ever again when I'm punishing someone, and I've told you to go upstairs?"

"No, Master."

Brian untied the girl. "Get out of here, and pray my slave's behavior improves. For your own sake."

She slid out of the chair as if she'd turned to liquid, then she crawled on shaking hands and knees out of the room.

Mina didn't speak as he untied her. He inspected her wrists, looking for chafing because God forbid she should suffer from something as terrible as chafing when he'd nearly turned her whipping girl into ribbons.

He led her down the hall to their room and pulled her into the bathroom. She tried to hold back the tears as he stripped her. "Sit and wait for me to call for you." He pointed at the bathtub in the corner.

He was already peeling his own clothing off. She tried not to stare at him. He was so beautiful on the outside, but on the inside, he was a wasteland.

Mina sat on the edge of the tub while Brian got in the shower. She watched as blood spattered the walls and swirled down the drain. When he was clean, he said, "Join me."

She was shaking when she got inside the shower. He ignored it and shackled her to the wall. He stared at her for a long time as the water ran off him. Then he began to work the soap into a lather between his hands. Then those soapy hands were on her, caressing and bathing. Instead of cleaning her body, she wished he could scrub the images of what had just happened in the cell from her mind.

He lingered over her breasts, kneading and rubbing them more than was necessary to get clean. Her body melted into his, surrendering as it always did. He spent an equally long time on her ass. Her breathing deepened as he stroked between her legs.

"Please don't do this," she whimpered. "Please stop making me feel things with you. I can't handle it anymore. I can't keep pretending I can deal with any of this."

He gripped her throat and stared into her eyes, daring her to close them and shut him out again. But she was too smart for that now. He might not beat her, but he'd shown he had no problem choosing someone to take her place.

"If you didn't disobey my clear orders this wouldn't have happened. It gives me no pleasure to see you tormented, but you will not defy me. You will obey me in all things no matter how small my command. Do you understand?"

"Yes, Master," she whispered.

Even if she were perfect it wouldn't matter. He'd still hurt others. He just wouldn't be doing it for her disobedience. She wouldn't be the direct cause of it. But he would do it. And she'd be forced to share a bed with him each night while he carefully stroked and kissed and licked her and she returned his favors. He would touch her as if she were hand-blown glass. Then he'd beat and fuck others like they were trash.

His lips pressed against hers in a kiss far too gentle for the anger he'd just unleashed. His hand cradled the back of her neck as he deepened it. And she let him. When his hand returned to caress between her legs, she spread them wider to give him greater access. And the worst of it was . . . it wasn't because she was afraid of him. It was because she needed his hands on her. She was addicted to the careful way he touched her. She was starved for it, and no amount of soft caressing would ever be enough to sate her need to be held and cared for. To feel something like the echo of love.

Brian pushed his fingers inside her, and she bucked against him. She didn't just open her legs for him, she opened her soul. He knelt between her legs while the water ran cold, stroking her with his tongue until she shuddered and came.

After it was over, he unshackled her and turned the water off. He wrapped a towel around his waist, and dried her off. He took her to bed and combed the tangles out of her hair. He held her forever, the only sound between them, their breathing.

"Make me come," he said.

She sucked his cock while he cooed in her ear about what a good girl she was and how pleased he was with her and how all was forgiven now. After he came, he drifted into sleep, his orgasm acting as a sedative.

Mina slipped out of the bed and dressed. There was still a tremor in her hand as she zipped and buttoned her jeans. She winced when she opened the door and it creaked, but he didn't stir.

Upstairs, whispers followed her as she passed through the lobby. They always followed her now, clinging to her like her shadow, refusing to ever detach and leave her in peace.

She wondered if she looked as flustered as she still felt. She felt shaky and weak, as if she hadn't eaten in a while. She needed to go outside to get some air. A few girls were in the heated pool, but it was mostly deserted. Mina looked out to the snow-covered woods, her gaze finding the place Annette had showed her, the hidden place just inside the property line. She wanted to go there and just stay and never come back—even if she froze. She started in that direction when Annette's voice stopped her.

"Mina, Lindsay told me what happened. Are you okay?"

Would everyone stop asking her that? No. She was not okay. And asking her a thousand more times wouldn't remedy the situation.

Mina turned, and suddenly all the emotion she'd been holding since she'd come back upstairs, spilled out of her. "No! I am not fucking okay. I have to get out of here. I have to leave. I don't care if the electric fence kills me. I'm going. Today. Now. I can't spend another minute with Brian in this house."

"I might be able to help," a male voice interrupted.

Mina had been so wrapped up in her own drama that she hadn't noticed the man and woman with Annette. They must be the guests Lindsay mentioned.

"This is Michael and his slave, Vivian," Annette said.

Vivian wore a platinum collar with aquamarine stones set inside the band. It must have cost a fortune. Mina felt a twinge of jealousy. The two of them seemed happy. He probably wasn't a psychopath. Why couldn't Mina have that? Why did it always have to be fucked-up sadists for her?

"You're Brian's slave?" Vivian asked, frowning.

God, had everybody in the known universe heard of Brian? Mina nodded.

"We will get you out," Michael said as if her future had been decided.

"He'd never let me go."

As if on cue, Brian walked up. So much for a dead sleep.

"I feel you when you aren't with me," he said. He sounded exhausted. "Do you want me to release you?"

Why did he have to seem so reasonable right now? So hurt that she could think to go? Mina looked away as Vivian took her arm and led her to stand behind Michael.

Brian turned his attention to the man. "And you're here to rescue her, I suppose? Is it a hobby of yours to keep women away from me?"

Mina closed her eyes and blocked it out while the two men yelled at each other. The words blended and merged together. All she could process was the anger. She thought it would come to blows until someone grabbed her. It was Brian.

"Do you want to leave with them?"

"You could be free again," Michael said.

Brian still looked hurt. She wanted to rage at him, yell like Michael had just yelled. How dare he have the nerve to be hurt after everything he did to others. She could have loved him. She could have been there for him if it weren't for the awful things he continued to do to people. The way he beat and fucked them and played sadistic mind games to break them.

"I-I can't do this anymore. I-it hurts too much."

His face darkened as if he were shutting down his emotions like one might shut off a computer. Just a press of a button. So simple.

"Fine," he said. He produced a key from his pocket and unlocked the collar, then he put the code in the metal band around her wrist and took that as well. "Get the fuck out," he said softly, "I never want to see you again."

He turned and walked away. He didn't spare her another glance as he flung the collar and bracelet against the wall and disappeared inside.

Mina stared after him. She felt numb. Jason had thrown her away just like this. Each man in her life had tormented and broken her into smaller pieces than the one before . . . and then they discarded her, tossed her away without a second look when they decided they'd had enough. But enough of what? Which of them had been made to suffer in all this? The men, or her?

No matter Brian's past, he still chose what he did to people. He was the one busy making victims.

Some insane part of her wanted to run after him, beg him to keep her. Because the moments with him when she'd been able to forget what he was and what he did in the dungeon cells had been everything she'd hoped a master could be. Gentle, patient. Pleasure, not pain. But his brutal nature . . . even if it wasn't pointed in her direction . . .

A hand gently touched her back, and her rescuers led her to her room downstairs. She wasn't sure where Brian had disappeared to, but he wasn't down there. She stood silently to the side while they packed up her things and took them outside to a waiting car with the aide of some of the men of the house. Despite the cold and the snow, the sun was shining. The sky was a crisp, sharp blue. She looked back to see the whipping girl standing in the doorway, seething with rage.

Vivian sat in the back of the car with her. Michael drove. That was when she snapped out of it. Wait, who were these people? Had she just lost her mind? Had she broken with reality? How would going off with strangers help anything?

"Let me go! I want to go back inside. I don't know you!"

Vivian put a hand over hers. "It's okay. I promise. We're friends with the partners."

Oh, that made it better.

"I can't imagine belonging to someone like Brian."

Vivian said his name with such disgust, it made Mina recoil further. Even while she agreed, a part of her couldn't help but want to defend him and the side of him she'd seen that the others hadn't.

Vivian started to search her, no doubt looking for wounds to bandage and soothe. Mina quickly pulled her shirt down when the woman took a peek at her back.

Vivian gasped. "Did he do that to you?"

"Do what?" Michael said from the front seat. He craned to try to see in the rear-view mirror.

She felt like such a sideshow. "No. Those were already there. Brian never left a mark on me."

Vivian seemed confused as if they must be talking about two different Brians.

"You can stay with us as long as you need to," Michael said. He met Vivian's eyes in the mirror, and they seemed to share some sort of understanding.

Mina looked out the back window as the large house was swallowed by the trees lining the road. And then they were driving down an old road in the middle of the woods, as if it had never existed at all.

"W-why are you helping me?" *Were* they helping her? Neither gave off the vibe Brian did. And neither seemed to have a personal interest in her. They were far too into each other to bring in a third. At least she hoped they were.

Mina wasn't sure how well they'd take rejection if they wanted her to play with them. The idea revolted her now. She couldn't do this shit again. Brian was the last one. Never again, no matter how good the offer sounded, it would always lead to this same pain. She should have chosen solitude from the beginning.

In his own way, Brian had been worse than Jason. Not just because he'd hurt someone else in front of her, but because she'd started to develop deeper caring for him, even when she knew she shouldn't. With Jason and those before him it had been the opposite. What started as an infatuation quickly turned to fear and loathing. With Brian, what started out as fear and loathing turned into fear and . . . something she didn't want to put a name to.

Mina looked back as the woods got smaller and smaller behind them. She touched her bare throat and tried not to miss the monster she'd just escaped.

Brian hid behind the broken TV. The dog whimpered nearby.

"Shut up!" he hissed. That stupid dog was going to get him found and beaten even worse for hiding from her.

"Where are you, you worthless little shit?" His stepmother's speech slurred as she moved nearer. She smelled of whiskey. The switch grazed over peeling wallpaper, then screeched against the glass of old picture frames. He cringed as the thick hickory switch slammed against a chair a few feet away. Dust flew up everywhere, and he started to cough.

"There you are. The good book says that if you spare the rod, you spoil the child. This is for your own good."

He fought and struggled against her, but she was strong for a woman, even drunk. Maybe she got stronger, drunk. Or less inhibited. The dog barked and snarled as she dragged Brian down the hallway. She kicked the dog, and he cried and whimpered and ran away. So much for canine protective urges. So much for man or boy's best friend.

Brian flinched as the switch came down over and over until it tore through his shirt, until it made him bleed, until the switch broke in half in the bitch's hand.

He tried to fight back, tried to get away, but she pressed him against the stairs. A cigarette dangled from her lips. It had dangled from her foul mouth since she'd started the beating. She took a long, slow drag, then twisted it out on his shoulder.

He howled as the cigarette sizzled on his skin and tried yet again to escape her. How could he be this weak? How could he let some *woman* do this to him? Finally, she threw him down on the ground, and he scrambled away.

"I'm going to lock you up again tonight!" she screamed after him. "Maybe the devil will come take you home. Maybe I'll leave you there for good until he does."

She'd already been starving him, keeping the food locked up and doling out just enough to keep him going. It was part of why he couldn't fight her. He was slowly getting taller, and with that would come more strength if she didn't find a way to balance it out. Starvation was only logical.

Brian ran to his room, thumbing through his mother's old records until he found the one he needed. He sat in the center of the bed, his knees drawn to his chest. The tears rolled down his cheeks as Chopin's soothing piano solos played.

The door opened, banging against the wall. She went straight for the record, scratching it as she ripped it from the turntable. "This same shit. Over and over and over. Don't you get sick of this stupid music? I should have taken it a long time ago."

He jumped off the bed to stop her. "No! You can't. Please, you can't take her from me! That's all I have left."

The photos of his mother had long been destroyed. He couldn't remember what she looked like. All he remembered was the smell of cookie dough and these records—this music.

"Please!" he screamed as his stepmother left the room. "Don't take her from me!"

She shoved him back and took the records outside to burn in a big trash can.

Brian bolted up in bed. He could still feel the heat of the flames from when he'd stood helpless watching what felt like his mother burning away. His hand shook as he turned on the bedside lamp, afraid he was still back there. But it was just him, alone in his room at the house.

Sleep had been much harder until he'd grown up and found the music again. It was a comfort to know that in nearly two hundred years, no fire had ever destroyed that music. It had survived. Like he had.

He'd grown bigger and stronger, ran away, gotten a job. It was only years later that he worked up the courage to face his stepmother again. By that point she seemed so small and helpless.

Hers was the first life he'd taken. After he'd finished, he'd cut her into pieces, burying them in different states. It was possibly foolish to have so much evidence scattered in so many places, but he'd convinced himself if he didn't separate the pieces, they'd only reassemble and come after him again.

After that, he'd slept soundly for a few months. But then the itch had started, and no amount of scratching would make it go away.

He wondered if he'd cried out or screamed in his sleep tonight. Instinctively, he wanted to reach out for Mina for comfort and to make sure she was okay . . . as if his stepmother could have stepped out of his dream and into hers to cause more carnage there. But he could see she wasn't here. Why hadn't he fought to keep her? Why had he let them take her? Michael couldn't have done a goddamn thing about it if he'd ordered her downstairs until they left.

And now the dreams were back.

He took a quick shower and put on a T-shirt and some sweatpants and tennis shoes. The house was quiet as he ascended into the main entryway. The lights were out except for the guide lights set low into the wall. He went out to the pool as if he might find Mina waiting for him to bring her back inside.

The collar and security bracelet were still on the ground where they'd fallen after he'd thrown them. He bent to pick up the collar and inspected it under the pool light. It was undamaged, which surprised him given how hard he'd thrown it. He went back inside and placed the collar in a box in his room. He couldn't destroy it. It was the only thing he had left of her.

When the collar was safely tucked away, he went back upstairs to the gym, put a Chopin CD in the sound system, and got on the treadmill. He didn't give a shit if he woke the whole house. If someone came in, they'd take one look at him, turn around, and walk back out. If they didn't, they'd wish to God they had because there was nothing he wanted more right now than to hurt someone.

When the dreams came, the only thing he wanted to do was run. Run from her, run from himself, run from everything, run from the monster that chased him, even when he was that monster. He didn't know who or what he ran from this time. But he was afraid nothing would stop his stepmother now.

For a while, hurting others had been enough, but then Mina was required. Without her, the dreams might never go away again. Without her, how could he make them stop?

Twelve

A week had passed since Brian released her. The dreams wouldn't stop. Every night they grew darker, more punishing, revealing everything he'd tried to keep buried deep within his psyche. Every night he reached out to hold Mina for her protection or his comfort he couldn't be sure. Maybe both. He became more erratic, punishing girls for looking at him the wrong way rather than waiting for them to be sent to him.

"Shut the door," Lindsay said, when he stepped into the shrink's office after being summoned like a child.

"Look, I know I'm more out of control than normal. It'll settle down in a few weeks." He had no idea what his fucked-up mind would do or how long it might take to *settle down*. "But you all need me. You can't run this operation without me, and you know it. And you can't exactly fire me."

"That's not why you're here," Lindsay said. He was drinking that pansy-ass camomile tea he always had brewing as if it somehow made him sophisticated and refined. As if he didn't have his own sadistic streak.

Just because it wasn't brought on by damage and trauma didn't mean it wasn't there.

"Then what do you want? I have bad sluts to punish."

"I need you to deal with Mina."

Brian's eyes narrowed. "What exactly do you mean by '*deal* with Mina'?" He had better not mean what Brian thought he meant.

"I mean deal with her. Vivian and Michael aren't keeping her locked up. They're just letting her wander around free. She has access to phones. She can leave them at any time. Once she gets her bearings she will go to the police and report all of us. I don't know if she could lead them directly here to the house, but she knows where my office is in the city. She knows where *Dome* is. We're trapped rats here if we don't handle her."

"No."

"Brian, I know you think you had some attachment to this girl, but she's dangerous to our survival."

"So much for all your fucking promises to her. You all think I'm the biggest monster here, but I don't lie about shit. Between my word and your word, anybody is safer with me and my word than with you and yours."

"If she hadn't come here and I thought she was a real threat and I'd sent you out to take care of the problem, you would have done it."

Brian remained stoic. He would neither confirm nor deny, but his gut said that no he wouldn't have. He had a vanishingly small circle of empathy, but somehow Mina had worked her way into it. She'd been protected the moment he'd seen her. If he'd been sent to kill her, no matter his original intention, something in her would have made him pause long enough to find the scars and the damage in her eyes that so mirrored his own. Then she would have gone immediately on the protect and defend list.

He ignored the voice in his head that accused him of destroying her anyway. Punishing others for her misbehavior to feed his ego and protect his reputation—even while he saw that it was damaging her. If he could go back . . . if he could undo that . . .

It was startling to feel regret.

It was such a foreign and uncomfortable emotion, he could barely stand to hold it in his mind. Everything he touched broke apart in his hands, even Mina. And if he tried to say anything different, he'd be a liar.

"If you won't do it . . ."

Brian stood and leaned over the desk. Lindsay visibly shrank back.

"Listen to me very carefully, asshole. I may have let her go, but Mina will always be under my protection. If you harm her in any way, if you send anyone else after her . . . If anything happens to her, I'm going to assume it was you, and then you will be on a very special, very short list of people whose body parts get lost in multiple states."

Before Lindsay could respond with anything intelligible—assuming he had anything intelligible to say—the phone rang.

The doctor picked it up, and Brian sat back down. He wasn't done here. Not by a long shot. He'd kill Lindsay right now if he couldn't reach some reasonable assurance that his threat would be heeded and Mina would remain safe.

There was frantic yelling on the other end of the phone with barely a breath between sentences.

"Vivian, I can't understand anything you're saying. You have to slow down."

Brian rolled his eyes, still wishing he'd truly gotten his hands on the precious princess Michael collared. Just once.

"What about Mina?" Lindsay said.

Brian lurched out of the chair and ripped the phone out of Lindsay's hand. "Vivian. Shut up."

The line sounded as if it had gone dead, but he knew better. "Tell me slowly and calmly what about Mina?"

"I—I—I . . ."

"I—I—I . . ." he mocked. "Spit it out or so help me I will drive to your house and drag the information out of you. And if your husband thinks he's got the balls to stop me, he can come right on ahead." He was spoiling for a fight. Any fight.

"How are you helping her to be more calm?" Lindsay asked.

Brian just glared.

A couple of minutes passed as Vivian collected herself. "M-Mina and I were shopping at an outdoor market. It was a safe area of town. I stepped away to another booth, and when I turned around, a black sedan had pulled up and some Asian men were shoving her into the back of the car. I-I couldn't get a license plate."

Brian hung up on her and turned to Lindsay. "Matsumoto has her. I told you there was something fucking wrong with him. Call the pilot and fuel up the jet."

"How did he know she was out? How could he have known where to find her?"

"I don't give a shit how he knew." He left the doctor gawking after him and went straight to the dungeons. He sorted through keys on a keyring until he found the one for the door inside his room. He slammed the lights on and smiled as he took in the rows and rows of guns, ammunition, knives, flashlights, body armor, grenades, and more interesting specialized toys for special circumstances.

Lindsay rushed in, out of breath, as Brian started dropping magazines, checking chambers, and packing a large black bag.

"What are you doing?"

Brian glared at the doctor as if he were the stupidest human being to ever walk the earth. "You know what I'm doing."

Mina felt like her head was stuffed with cotton as the room came into focus.

"There she is. You Americans are so delicate. You've been in and out for the past day."

She had the vaguest recollection of waking in the presence of strange men a couple of times. Voices had faded back out as soon as they'd faded in, and then everything had gone away again. It had felt like tendrils of odd dreams trying to string themselves together. She'd heard sounds in those brief moments that she now knew had been a plane. She was only now awake enough to realize things had gotten very bad for her.

Just when she'd thought she was free.

She was far outside the hope of safety or freedom now. Even without a collar around her throat or an electronic leash or any type of binding, she knew she'd never been more truly bound than she was at this moment.

A short, but still somehow very frightening Japanese man came into focus above her. His accent was thick, but his words had been clearly spoken.

"That's the fucking *Gaijin* whore you were going to pay one and a half million for?"

Mina's head swiveled to the left to see another man in the room. Larger, also Japanese. He looked like a bodyguard and probably was.

She scrambled to a seated position as her eyes continued to adjust to the light. The room had the sparse, minimalism of a zen garden. There was a bright red mattress and bedding on the floor. Meditation pillows sat in a row next to a short, square table. Lamps lit the space. The floor was bamboo with rugs on top. The room had sliding doors that were pale cream and looked translucent like fine quality paper.

"Do not let the room mislead you. You're in a cell underground. There is stone surrounding the outside of this oasis. You will not be allowed to wander the property unescorted. This will be your room, and you will call me Master."

It had to be another dream. The implausibility of landing back in another sadistic master's hands without even seeking it out was too much.

A crack sounded as the back of his hand connected with her face. The sting seemed to come years later, but it arrived with a crushing brutality that stole the breath from her lungs and sent her to a crouched position.

"Say it," he demanded.

"M-Master."

"Good."

"H-how . . . w-why . . ." She cringed as his face darkened at the words she hadn't been able to keep under wraps.

"You were greatly resented at the house. One girl overheard a conversation where my name was mentioned. After being punished for you, she reflected on the conversation and stole my contact information. She called after you left. The only thing she asked was that I make you pay for the suffering you caused her. To be truthful, I don't care about her suffering, but I do like to hurt people, so granting her request is no burden. I would have done it anyway."

He clapped his hands together in two sharp snaps. The doors slid open, and a couple of men brought in familiar dungeon equipment.

The men set up the equipment, then brought in a box of whips and shackles and riding crops. They slid the doors shut again on their way out.

The man now known only as her master, stared at Mina as if he were trying to decide if she'd been worth the trip to pick up, even though no money had exchanged hands. She didn't beg him. She could already tell by the hard glint in his eyes that begging would only excite him more. It was the look Brian got when dealing with other women in the house, and no amount of begging had ever resulted in mercy from him.

Her new master would force it out of her when things got bad and she was desperate and babbling just to prove to herself she was still alive.

How long that might be the case, she wasn't sure. After all, this man hadn't invested anything in her. Had he actually paid all of that money, she might have the hope of long term survival. Not that she thought that would be a better outcome at the hands of a sadist.

Her ring was gone. Of course he wouldn't let her keep it, but could he know it was one of the few physical objects that meant anything to her? Only her collar had come to mean as much. But Brian had taken that.

All at once she started to cry. She cried for the foolish decision to try to escape Brian when she'd already begun to miss him as they were pulling away from the house. She cried for his rejection and how coolly and easily he'd tossed her aside. She cried for the jealousy and pain that crawled up her throat trying to choke her from the inside as she'd watched Michael and Vivian the past few days, seeing how happy they were, how healthy their dynamic was, wondering why it couldn't be her. Finally, she cried for the fate she'd been sealed into as if bricked in behind a wall piece by piece where no one would ever find her.

Her new master watched as she wore herself out. He hadn't laid a hand on her yet, and surely he must think all of her tears were for him. She hoped to cry herself out so almost none of them would remain for him to claim as his own.

He clapped again—this time, once. The doors slid open again, and in walked another American girl. But her style of clothing was more Japanese. The fabric was transparent, and Mina could see the other woman's breasts and bare mound. A dragon tattoo snaked it's way around her belly, gently touching the top of her pubic bone as if it might crawl down just a few inches to tease an orgasm from her.

The girl knelt in front the man who'd summoned her. "Yes, Master?" She brushed her lips over his bare feet and waited. There were deep purple bruises around her throat and wrists. And it looked as if she'd been recently beaten.

"Meet your replacement."

"N-no, Master, please. Please keep me. Whatever I did . . . I'm sorry to offend." Her next words were a string of unintelligible Japanese.

Somehow Mina didn't think the other girl wanted to stay because she liked him so much—more likely she only wanted to live.

"Bring me the tapestry," he said.

She disappeared out the door and came back with an elegant, embroidered white tapestry. She spread it out under a Saint Andrew's Cross the men had placed against one wall.

"You may go. Use this time wisely to find a way to convince me to keep you instead of the new whore."

She made a small, dignified bow, having seemed to collect herself, and made her way to the door. The bodyguard gave her a long once-over, his fingertips brushing over hers as she left. The movement wasn't noticed by the master, but it was significant to Mina. It was a crushing blow, that even here in this place with this cruel man, the other American girl had found someone to show her kindness, perhaps even love.

The bodyguard's hard gaze went back to Mina, leaving no doubt that his softer expression wouldn't extend to her.

The master circled Mina, observing her. "Do you know your name means *love*?"

She shook her head.

"How ironic that you appear to be so unlovable at the hands of every man who touches you." He paused, seeming to enjoy dragging out her torment. "Do you know what the tapestry is for?"

Again, she shook her head. It earned her another hard slap.

"No, Master," he said, sharply.

"N-no, Master."

"You will spill blood for me tonight. You will spill it many nights. You'll spill it on that tapestry, and then I will hang it on this wall. When every wall is covered in these tapestries, the full weight of your enslavement to me will have sunk in."

Brian crouched behind a bush on a hilltop two hundred yards from the house. Matsumoto's property stretched for thirty acres or more. Brian had already taken out the few patrolling guards outside. He'd made an extra few circuits over the path he'd watched them walk to ensure no more were coming.

When he was sure it was only him and the local wild-life, he set up equipment. He'd had night-vision goggles on since he'd reached the property. He took them off to switch out the batteries, then put a suppressor on the sniper rifle.

He'd picked this spot because there was a large flat rock and a clear view of the house. It was as if Matsumoto had gifted him with it specifically to eliminate his men and take down his well-guarded fortress. Perhaps the man had a guilty conscience and was begging for pain to absolve him of his misdoings. Brian was happy to oblige him.

He adjusted the scope on the rifle. He'd considered cutting the power and going in and doing a clean sweep, but Matsumoto's men would have night-vision goggles or a backup generator. Cutting the power was what you did on a B&E in middle class neighborhoods where people were too comfortable to understand the street but too poor to be able to afford much in the way of tactical equipment.

Brian shot out the two video cameras on the front of the house—and the one on the side—from his perch. Then he waited.

Predictably, two men spilled out the front door to investigate the sound of shattered glass. They must not get visitors like this often. Had it been Brian, he would have gone to the control room and checked the surveillance screens to make sure the video feed was operational before walking right out the front door like a bright and shining target.

He eliminated the two guards and waited. When they didn't return to their posts, more would arrive. He grabbed his bag and changed his position. The next three that came out were smarter than the first two. They were armed and crept around the side of the house, thinking whoever was out there was still at the front.

Nice try but not good enough. Brian killed the first two as they crept around the side of the building. The third spun around and shot into the night. Brian flattened himself against the ground as the bullet whizzed by. He returned fire.

And then there were none.

Except that wasn't quite right. There were always more. Especially with a guy as paranoid as Matsumoto. Brian almost had to respect that level of paranoia.

He made his way closer to the back of the house, then pulled a grenade from his bag. It had a fifteen meter blast radius. He moved far enough away to ensure he wouldn't get the house. Minutes after the explosion went off, all the rest of Matsumoto's little army men came pouring out the back door. Right in the direction of the explosion.

Idiots. For a man with so much money, Matsumoto could afford to hire a better security detail. He lobbed the second grenade at the same place as the first, and body parts went everywhere.

By now Matsumoto knew someone was coming. Brian could have crept around the house like a ninja, taking them one by one, but the risk was higher that way, and if he didn't keep himself alive, he'd be of no use to Mina.

He slipped the smaller guns and knives and extra magazines into various holsters, leaving nothing behind that could be turned on him, later. Except the rifle, which he hid along with the bag.

He walked in through the front door. If anyone beyond Matsumoto remained in the house, they knew he was coming, though they'd probably still default to the expectation he'd try a side entrance because it was more covert. Brian had given up covert with the grenades, but he'd saved himself a lot of work. He screwed a suppressor on his .22 and stepped inside.

He was down to servants huddled in corners. This was the group that begged—the group who thought he might spare them. But that wasn't how this went. Witnesses were a no go, and it was impossible to tell which intrepid cook or maid might sneak up on him later to try to be a hero.

He took them out one by one. Unarmed fish in barrels. At the back of the house were a set of stairs that went down into what he could only assume were Matsumoto's dungeons. Even below ground they would have heard the explosion above. It wasn't as if grenades were subtle.

But he'd cleared the main floor, and it was the only place remaining. Brian had left empty magazines all over Matsumoto's home. He holstered the gun and pulled out a larger caliber.

He crept down the stairs. It was silent, but he wasn't fooled. He checked each room in turn until he got to the one at the end. He kicked the door in and leaped out of the way in case a bullet was coming. Even with body armor, he wasn't taking chances. Instead, a throwing star came at him at just the right angle to get his shoulder. Motherfucker!

He stormed in, infuriated and caught a bullet in his vest. A few inches another way, and he might be in trouble. He returned fire, and took the bodyguard out with two in the neck. Elsa screamed and threw herself on top of the man. Brian remembered her from her time in the house.

Matsumoto stood behind Mina with a knife to her throat. She was tied naked to a Saint Andrew's Cross and bleeding. She appeared unconscious already. Maybe dead. He tried to shut out that last possibility.

As if reading his mind, Matsumoto said, "I just whipped her unconscious. She's not dead."

He moved closer and looked her over. There was too much blood. He grasped her hand. Her ring was gone, probably taken off her. She always wore it.

Brian felt himself go cold. The rage and indignation he'd felt when the throwing star had nicked him was forgotten. Now he was really angry. The kind of angry that got quiet and still and felt like a subzero freezer. The kind of angry that doubled back until there was no discernible emotion to be detected anywhere.

He shrugged. "What do I care if she's alive or not. I came here to kill you for stealing our property and obviously breaking the contract you would have signed had you bought her properly. Kill her, don't kill her. Either way, you're a dead man."

Matsumoto must have bought the bluff because he darted to steal the fallen bodyguard's gun, but he couldn't get to it in time before Brian shot him in the leg and took him down. He didn't want him dead yet.

He grabbed the man and flung him over a spanking horse and shackled him to it. Brian rushed to Mina and felt for a pulse. He breathed a sigh of relief when he found it steady and stronger than expected.

"Elsa," he said.

She looked up, her face tear streaked and angry. "What?"

He took in the marks Matsumoto had left on her. "Why didn't you tell us he was abusing you during our check ins?"

"He was patient. He didn't start until the check-in visits stopped. By then I was too afraid of him."

Elsa spoke in a reasonable manner, but there was murderous intent in her eyes for killing the man that was obviously her lover.

"I can't let you go. You're a loose end. You're too damaged to resell, and you'd be a liability at the house."

"Mina will never forgive you if you kill me," she said.

"She's unconscious. She'll never know what happened here." He killed Elsa quickly and cleanly, and then untied Mina. She slumped against him, the blood still dripping down her back onto a white tapestry.

"So you're killing everyone but me? To send a message?" Matsumoto asked.

"Oh, no, I'm killing you. You'll die in the fire."

He took Mina outside and retrieved the gasoline he'd discovered in a nearby outbuilding during his initial sweeps. He went through every room, dousing the house —especially Matsumoto. When he and Mina were a safe distance away, he lit it.

Thirteen

Mina cringed when she felt the hand on her face. She wanted nothing more than to slip back into the grace of unconsciousness to step outside of this place and away from her new horrible master. She wanted this deceptively kind touch to be Brian's. She wished it so fervently that she could almost smell him and believe.

"Mina."

The sound of loud engines woke her more fully. When she opened her eyes, she found she was lying down with her head on Brian's lap. His shirt was off, and there was a bandage on his shoulder. As she grew more lucid she could feel the bandages on her own back. And the pain. She felt the cool metal of the collar around her throat. She couldn't see it, but reaching to touch it, she knew it was Brian's. Matsumoto hadn't put a collar on her.

This wasn't happening. It was a dream. A lovely dream. If she let herself believe this was real and then woke up . . .

"Drink." The cool water sliding down her throat finally convinced her she was really with him.

"We're going back to the house." His tone brooked no argument, but she wouldn't have argued. She would have begged to go back with him. She couldn't believe he'd come for her. She'd been sure she would die in there. Maybe she *was* dead.

"I shouldn't have released you. But I shouldn't have tortured that girl in front of you, either." Mina lay silently listening to him speak as he stroked her hair. "I don't know how normal emotions work. I don't know why you're an exception that lets me feel something almost like a real feeling. I don't know if I love you or if I'm capable of it, but you are *mine*. You will always be mine. In the future I will consider all the ways I could damage you, not just the ways prohibited in a contract. And I will protect you from those things. That's the best I can offer, but I need your obedience, and I need you to understand that I'm too broken to ever fix. I am what I am, but you are under my protection. That has to be enough. Is that enough for you?"

It wasn't enough. It should be, but it wasn't. But it didn't matter because whether it was packaged in the way she thought it should be, Lindsay had delivered to her exactly what he'd promised and what she'd asked for: a master who would be gentle with her and respect her boundaries.

"Yes, Master," she said. It was a lie, but it didn't matter. Everything he'd asked was rhetorical. He wouldn't let her go again. Not ever. She could feel the weight of self-blame on him for releasing her and his determination to keep her this time. It was explicitly stated in the grip he kept on her waist as if she might levitate up and away from him.

"We don't know how he found you."

Mina tensed.

"But you do." It was scary how little it was possible to hide from him, no matter how badly she wanted to. "Tell me." It wasn't a request.

"The girl you punished in my place before you let me go . . ."

"Cate?"

Was that her name? She hadn't known.

"She knew he bid on me but that you'd taken the bid from him because of something Lindsay said. She broke into Lindsay's office and found the man's number."

The look that spread across Brian's face was so dark and hard, she almost regretted telling him the truth. She didn't ask what he'd done at the Japanese man's house, if he'd killed everyone, if he'd left any survivors. She doubted it, but she didn't want to know, and she was afraid if she asked he might tell her.

"Rest. We've got a long flight," he said.

That was no problem. She was certain she could sleep for the rest of her life if she made the smallest effort. The last thing she realized as sleep claimed her was that she could feel the weight of her grandmother's ring on her finger.

Many hours later she woke in Brian's bed. There was a tray of food on the nightstand. "You need to eat something. You need fluids, especially. I brought you soup, but you can have anything else in the kitchen after that."

"Thank you for coming for me. And for finding my ring."

He rested a hand against her cheek and nodded.

"I'm going to deal with Cate now. Don't interfere. Just be grateful if I decide to leave her breathing when I'm done."

Mina felt a coldness seep into her bones and spread to her extremities. She felt something flip over inside of her, a dark thing that she'd pushed aside each time before when she'd been hurt or misused.

It itched.

Her gaze rose to Brian. "I don't care what you do to her."

He smiled and pressed a kiss to Mina's forehead. "That's my girl. I knew you were in there somewhere."

He lingered and held her gaze, a long moment of understanding passing between them. They were too broken—both of them—clinging to each other at sea on a raft that would never reach land.

Brian squeezed her hand and left. Minutes later Cate's screams filled the hallway. Mina looked to the door then back at her food and finished her dinner.